Fountain
and
Tomb

Fountain and Tomb

(Hakayat Haretna)

Naguib Mahfouz

translated from the Arabic by
Soad Sobhy
Essam Fattouh
James Kenneson

Winner of the 1986 Arab League Translation Award

An Original from Three Continents

©1988 James Kenneson, Soad Sobhy, and Essam Fattouh

First English-language edition

Three Continents Press, Inc.
1636 Connecticut Avenue, N.W.
Washington, D.C. 20009

Portions of this translation appeared
previously in *Antaeus, The Michigan
Quarterly Review, The Missouri
Review,* and *Ploughshares.*

Library of Congress Cataloging-in-Publication Data

Maḥfūẓ, Najīb, 1912-
   Fountain and Tomb.

    Translation of: Hikāyāt hāratinā.
    Bibliography: p.
    I. Title. II. Title: Hakayat haretna.
PJ7846.A46H5413   1988   892'.736   86-51004
ISBN 0-89410-580-9
ISBN 0-89410-581-7 (pbk.)

Cover and illustrations by Max Winkler
©1988 Three Continents Press

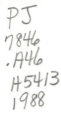
Introduction

The popularity of the fiction of Naguib Mahfouz in Egypt and the Arabic-speaking world can hardly be exaggerated. His work is read by the barely literate and the highly educated alike, and his name is a household word. Yet not one of the forty or so novels and story collections he has written since 1938 could be considered in any sense "popular fiction." Though his style is accessible and his delight in telling a good story obvious, Mahfouz has never stopped experimenting with formal patterns and techniques and has consistently avoided giving facile or self-serving answers to the difficult philosophical and political questions he raises: How can a man be happy? Is evil made by men or is it part of the structure of things? What do society and individual owe each other and why are they so often in conflict? How and why do cultures change? When values are being transformed, what is right? How much influence should tradition, religion, and politics exert on our lives? How shall we live both among others and within ourselves? Depicting his characters' attempts to resolve these universal problems while caught in the densely intricate web of Egyptian culture has been his lifelong project.

Mahfouz traces his interest in writing to early childhood and acknowledges political and literary debts to his father, a government clerk whose devotion to the heroes of independence from British rule— Saad Zaghloul, Mohamed Farid, Mostafa Kamel—fired the imagination of the youngest of his seven children. Born in 1911 in the El-Gamaliya district of Old Cairo, Naguib Mahfouz witnessed the upheavals of war, martial law, the rebellion of 1919, the deportation of Saad Zaghloul in 1921, the stormy promulgation of the unsatisfactory constitution of 1923, the return of Zaghloul from exile, and his death in

1

1927, events which provide the political context of *Fountain and Tomb*. The literary side of the debt comes from frequent visits to the family home by the journalist and satirist El-Muwaylili, whose *Hadith Issa Ibn Hisham,* sometimes considered a forerunner of the novel in Egypt, was dedicated to Mahfouz' father.

Both parents were devout Moslems. Their decision to send Naguib to mosque school at an early age influenced the prose style of the adult writer and probably contributed to his portrayal of many characters with an interest in Sufism, which he uses to represent a desire to withdraw from a world embroiled in conflicts and sick with divided loyalties. But the retreat into religion never works out for Mahfouz' characters; his mind is primarily a philosophical one, never ceasing to question, never finding a point of complete rest, not even in a balance of opposites.

Mahfouz' preoccupation with philosophy dates to his high-school days. Even then, the Islamic thinker Al-Akkad was one of his heroes. When he graduated from high school, Mahfouz was torn between literary and philosophical studies but finally decided to enter the Philosophy Department of Cairo University. During his student years he contributed both philosophical articles and short stories to periodicals. He still considers the day one of his stories was accepted by *Magalit El-Ruwayya* (*Story Magazine*) the most important of his life.

Mahfouz' early writing established him as a pioneer of the Arabic novel. Fiction was adopted relatively late by a culture which had long distrusted the novel and the theater in favor of poetry, traditionally perceived as the quintessentially "natural" form of literary expression. The experiments in fiction of Taha Hussein and Mohamed Heykal during the Arab cultural renaissance that began at the turn of the century found their fruition in the works of Mahfouz, who attacked and solved the formal and stylistic problems that had plagued the novel's earliest Arabic practitioners.

Mahfouz creates and inhabits many worlds in his fiction, but the center of his universe is the narrow zigzag streets, packed with activity, where he spent his early childhood. Though his family moved to the Abbasiyya district in 1924, Mahfouz' attachment to Gamaliya has persisted. He can still be seen visiting El-Hussayn and Al-Azhar or sitting with a new generation of writers in the cafes of the area. There he continues to study the complex lives of the lower-middle and lower-class people of the district whose world, without their wholly conscious knowledge, is changing rapidly. Socio-economic and political transformations in the wider world exist for the alley's inhabitants only when they touch an individual living there. Then, and not until then, do they become news.

This is the milieu Mahfouz is most consistently and strongly attracted to, but the instant popularity of his early (1945-1947) works dealing with alley and suburb (*El Qahira El-Gedida* [*New Cairo*], *Khan El-Khalili,* and *Midaq Alley*), which led to films and TV serials and which endure to this day, may have been partly responsible for leading him to use the same setting to create a recognized masterpiece of Arabic fiction, the trilogy (*Bain El Qasrain, Qasr El Shoq,* and *El Sokkeria*). Modeled in part on the works of Tolstoy and Dostoevski, the trilogy covers four decades of Egyptian social life, and Egyptian culture is its hero and heroine. The work's best-known character, the domineering El Sayed who suppresses his devout and humble wife, has become a national legend and a part of Egyptian folklore.

This trilogy, Mahfouz' most ambitious work, provides a fine example of his structural expertise. The first volume is the longest and most detailed, yet covers the shortest period of time, while the third and shortest has a simpler, faster style and covers the longest period. In this structure and other techniques that support it, the work embodies not only the change but also the acceleration of the pace of change in Egyptian culture.

Other notable innovations Mahfouz has brought to Arabic fiction include the use of first- and third-person stream-of-consciousness and his development of dialogue that maintains the easy rhythms of colloquial speech while remaining firmly in the tradition of the classical literary language. His explorations of the possibilities of the fantastic and the allegorical show an acknowledged American influence, that of Melville, and some of his more abstract short stories can only be called *littérature des idées* in the vein of Camus and Sartre.

As a pioneer of the novel of social criticism in a country where successive governments—the monarchy under the British thumb or the post-1932 republic—have readily resorted to censorship, Mahfouz has often found his work the subject of controversy. The works *Tharthara foq El Nil* (*Chatter on the Nile*), *Miramar,* and *El Hob Tahti El Matar* (*Love in the Rain*) caused him the most political trouble. The long allegory of science and religion, *Awlad Haretna* (published in English as *Children of Gebelawi*), aroused such a storm while running as a serial that it could not be printed in book form in Egypt, but it did eventually come out in Beirut.

Even when political or religious themes are central, however, Mahfouz is always concerned with broader issues: the nature of evil and virtue in their concrete manifestations, the moral dilemmas of individuals in a society afflicted by war and oppression, and the contrast between he who acts against society and he who struggles and

3

suffers on its behalf. Over all these hangs the modern predicament: not everything that happens in the world is rational or understandable through science or logic, but religion and all other systems of belief and value appear to be, at best, comforting mirages.

All Mahfouz' major themes and techniques find a place in *Fountain and Tomb,* a novel disguised as a collection of tales. (The literal translation of the title is "Tales of Our Quarter.") Characteristic motifs are interwoven to form striking patterns, new aspects of themes are illuminated by later tales, and stories are juxtaposed for both reinforcement and contrast, as in the case of the sisters Fathaya and Somaya or of the gang leaders, each remembered in the alley in different ways. The physical structures of the alley provide a symbolic world through which the characters unwittingly move. At its wide end, the alley debouches into a large square leading to the infinite possibility of Cairo, Egypt, and the world; at the other, it goes through an archway to the restful square and garden of the Sufi *takiya* and then becomes a narrow path to the cemetery and the tombs of ancestors. Evil spirits lurk in the archway, enemies from neighboring alleys in the great square. Between the two, in the mosques, cafes, businesses and homes, daily routine goes on, the fountain and all it represents at its center.

Mahfouz renders the most violent, touching, and grotesque incidents in a non-judgmental tone, that of the naive voice of a child. In a society rigidly segregated by sex and class, as Egypt was in 1920, a child may enter where an adult cannot. Thus the wide-eyed narrator spies on a *zar,* or rite of exorcism, attended only by women; adults chat uninhibitedly before him about birth and adultery; from his roof he witnesses fights, lovers' meetings, a woman sunbathing under a skylight, and a political demonstration; a nationalist group even takes advantage of his innocence to trick him into distributing anti-British pamphlets.

But the perspective often shifts, sometimes clearly, sometimes subtly, to that of an adult reflecting upon childhood memories, introducing a deliberate ambiguity about where reality ends and illusion takes over, about what the child knew at the time and what the adult reasoned out much later. In addition, the voice of the child is often filtered through much more sophisticated voices. Mahfouz uses the ancient intonation of the marketplace storyteller and the raucous snarl of the inveterate gossip to increase the thematic range and ambiguity of the tales. He then adds yet another dimension of tonal modulation by employing a variety of techniques, forms, and stances. While many stories are realistic, romantic, or lyrical, others are symbolic, minimalist, or just plain peculiar. Mahfouz has brought his whole arsenal to

4

bear on this slender volume, seventy-eight tales in fewer than two hundred pages, unified in complex and fascinating ways. In its intelligent manipulation of both ancient and ultramodern ideas about fictions, *Fountain and Tomb* is experimental in the best sense. Though published over ten years ago, it is still far ahead of much that passes for experimental in the West, and its themes, which are not constituted by its own techniques but served by them, make far more human reading.

The theme of transition central to most of Mahfouz' work is here symbolized by the initiation of a child into a great and vastly complicated society which is itself in flux. As the child's understanding grows and as the perspective of the older man enriches our knowledge of cultural changes, we, too, are initiated into Egyptian culture and the narrator's multiple views of it. The careful reader can learn more about Egyptian society and its values from this small book than he could from several dozen volumes of history and anthropology, a fact of no small importance in a world where misunderstandings among nations grow wider by the week and in a West where the writings of such authors as Mahfouz are seldom translated and almost never read. We learn what it was like in the old days and, by implication or outright statement, what it is like now. Skepticism enters the alley in the person of a free-thinking schoolteacher. The whole district is scandalized when a young woman takes a job as a government clerk, but it is clear that such behavior is soon to become acceptable and proper. One day a gang leader dies and no one rises up to take his place; the order of society has changed and a local tyrant is no longer needed. A sheikh once revered as a fortune-teller wanders into beggary in a less gullible age. There are rumors that the Sufi monastery will be torn down to make way for urban development, an action unthinkable only a few years earlier.

But it is clear that the people of the alley never stop living in a God-centered world. Even thugs and deadbeats justify themselves in religious terms, and the name of Allah rises constantly to people's lips. At the same time, their beliefs are subtly undercut and questioned by the narrator's real or illusory encounter with the High Sheikh of the *takiya*. Is God real or not? The question, raised in the opening tale, lingers at the close of *Fountain and Tomb* in the adult's puzzled memories and hangs over the novel like the archway and its *afreets* over the alley itself. The reader is left groping, like the narrator, or stumbling around in circles, like the blind man and the drunk, to find the right way to understand the *takiya,* the right way to move toward it and the tomb beyond. Typically, Mahfouz implies the question, but never forces it upon the reader or attempts to supply a definitive answer.

Though the fiction of Naguib Mahfouz is sometimes described as

5

detached, his is not the detachment of cold-bloodedness or indifference. His stories celebrate love, commitment, and, above all, wonder, especially at the dreams men live by:

> The dream is what matters. God gave them the gift of the dream. Do you have a dream . . . ?

S. S., E. F., J. K., 1986

A Note on Transliteration

No attempt has been made to transliterate Arabic letters and sounds into their supposed English equivalents, complete with diacritical paraphernalia. Words and names have been spelled to approximate Egyptian pronunciation as closely as possible without cluttering the text. So, while the apostrophe in "So'ad" is needed to make it sound like "so odd" rather than "toad," nothing is needed to make the English reader come close to the proper pronunciation of "Saad." Also, in the interest of simplicity, the prefix "Al" has been dropped before some of the many last names to be found in *Fountain and Tomb*.

Bibliography

Works by Naguib Mahfouz Available in English

Autumn Quail. Cairo: American University in Cairo Press, 1985.
Children of Gebelawi. Translated by Philip Stewart. London: Heine-
mann Educational Books, 1981.
God's World. An anthology of short stories translated by Akef Abadir
and Roger Allen. Minneapolis: Biblioteca Islamica, 1973.
Midaq Alley. Translated by Trevor Le Gassick. London: Heinemann
Educational Books, 1975.
Miramar. Translated by Fatma Moussa-Mahmoud, revised and edited
by Maged el Kommus and John Rodenbeck. London and Cairo:
Heinemann Educational Books in conjunction with American
University in Cairo Press, 1978.
Mirrors. Translated by Roger Allen. Minneapolis and Chicago: Biblio-
teca Islamica, 1977.
The Thief and the Dogs. Translated by M.M. Badawi and Trevor Le
Gassick, revised by John Rodenbeck. Cairo: American Univer-
sity in Cairo Press, 1985.
Wedding Song. Translated by Olive E. Kenny, revised by Mursi Saad
El Din and John Rodenbeck. Cairo: American University in
Cairo Press, 1985.

Selected Critical Works

Allen, Roger. *The Arabic Novel, An Historical and Critical Introduction.* Syracuse, N.Y.: Syracuse University Press, 1982.

Kilpatrick, Hilary. *The Modern Egyptian Novel: A Study in Social Criticism.* London: Ithaca Press, 1974.

Moosa, Matti. *The Origins of Modern Arabic Fiction.* Washington, D.C.: Three Continents Press, 1983.

Peled, Mattityahu. *Religion, My Own: The Literary Works of Naguib Mahfouz.* New Brunswick, N.J.: Transaction Books, 1983.

Somekh, Sasson. *The Changing Rhythm: A Study of Naguib Mahfouz' Novels.* Leiden: E.J. Brill, 1973.

1

I enjoy playing in the small square between the archway and the takiya where the Sufis live. Like all the other children, I admire the mulberry trees in the takiya garden, the only bit of green in the whole neighborhood. Our tender hearts yearn for their dark berries. But it stands like a fortress, this takiya, circled by its garden wall. Its stern gate is broken and always, like the windows, shut. Aloof isolation drenches the whole compound. Our hands stretch toward this wall— reaching for the moon.

Once in a while one of the longbeards appears in the garden in a bright, patterned skullcap and a huge rippling cape, and then we all yell, "If God wills, you dervish, you might get your wish."

But he just gazes at the grass and goes on, pausing, perhaps, beside the garden's small stream before vanishing behind the inner gate.

"Father, who are those men?"

"They are the men of God." And then in a very meaningful tone, "Damned be anyone who disturbs their peace."

But I still burn for those mulberries.

One day, tired of playing, I sit down to rest and immediately begin dozing. I wake to an empty square; even the sun has gone into hiding behind the ancient wall. The spring scene fades, heavy with the breath of sunset. I have to get away from the archway and back to our alley before it's pitch dark, so I jump up, ready to go. But then comes the uncanny feeling that I'm not alone, that I'm roaming in some pleasant magnetic field. When a warm breeze flows over me, I peer toward the takiya.

There, under the central mulberry tree, stands a man, a dervish unlike those I've seen before. He is great with age but extremely tall, his face a pool of glowing light. His cape is green, his long turban white. Everything about him is munificent beyond imagining. I look at him so intently that I become intoxicated, the sight of him filling the whole universe. It comes to me that he must be the owner and overseer of the place, and I see that he is loving, not like those others. I go up to the wall and say most respectfully, "I love mulberries."

Since he doesn't answer, doesn't even move, I assume he hasn't heard me, so I say it louder. "I love mulberries."

I believe that his single glance takes in everything and that his deep, melodious voice says, "My nightingale, *khoon deli khord wakuli hasel kared.*"

Then I think I see him tossing me a berry. I bend down to pick it up. I find nothing. When I stand up again, the place is empty. Darkness veils the inner gate.

Of course I tell my father the whole thing. He glares at me doubtfully. I tell it all over again. He says, "Your description doesn't fit anyone but the High Sheikh himself, but he never leaves his retreat."

On all the names of God, I swear I'm telling the truth; I even repeat the words of the sheikh. My father says, "I wonder what this gibberish you've memorized could mean."

"I've heard it before in the chanting from the takiya."

My father broods for a while before saying, "Don't tell a soul about this." He spreads his hands and recites the sura of the Oneness of the Eternal.

I dash back across the square and wait about till all the other children are gone. I expect the sheikh to appear, but he doesn't. In my thin voice, I call out, "My nightingale, *khoon deli khord wakuli hasel kared.*"

No answer. I ache with expectation, but he takes no pity on my desire to see him. Mulling over the event much later, I wonder about its reality. Did I really see the sheikh or just pretend I did to get attention—and then end up believing my own fantasy? Did I merely see a drowsy mirage and then make the daydream real from stories about the High Sheikh I'd heard around the house? It seems it must have been something like that since the sheikh never appeared again and since everyone agreed that he never came outside.

That's how I created a myth and then destroyed it—except that this supposed vision of the sheikh burrowed deep down into my very marrow, a memory of great purity. And except that I'm still crazy about mulberries.

2

The morning sun stretches out in the clear sky. My spot on our roof gives me a view of many minarets and domes, and I spy on a crow perched on the clothesline peg stuck into the wall along the roof. The mere sight of our neighbor's roof makes my mouth water, and I get the urge to pay a little visit on Zaki's mother and see if there's anything sweet around. I hop over the low wall and walk to her skylight. I peek through a broken pane and see the good lady Um Zaki positioned precisely beneath the skylight, utterly naked. She's sunbathing on her sofa and combing her hair, utterly naked, a strange and astonishing sight since she's as big as a cow. I yell, "Hi, Auntie!"

She's panic-stricken until she looks up and sees who it is. Then she chuckles and yells right back at me, "You little devil! Get down here!"

I hurry down but pull up short at her door, polite and puzzled. I ask myself out loud, "Am I supposed to go in?"

She overhears me and tells me I should , so I go in. As I approach the sofa, she smiles and says, "I've got you this time, you sneaky little hero, you." Then she flops down on her stomach and demands, "Rub my back."

Happy to oblige, I roll my sleeves up and set to work with enthusiasm. While I breathe the aroma of her flesh, saturated with soap and oil of cloves, she murmurs, "God bless your hands" and "You're a demon from paradise!" Still chuckling, she says, "The smart chicken hatches and knows all the catches: straight from the shell, he starts raising hell."

I apply myself with even greater zeal and she cries, "Hey, get your hands up a bit higher, you Satan. Going to tell your mother?"

"Never."

She giggles and exclaims, "So you even know that certain things are better left unsaid! You really are a devil. Did you learn massage in mosque school? What *do* you learn there, anyway?"

"The Exordium and the alphabet."

"May Allah preserve you, and I'll come to you when you're a beautician. What's for lunch today?"

"Okra."

"Fantastic! I'll eat at your house."

Her visits are gay and funny; countless jokes pour out of her, even dirty jokes. My mother tries to shoo me away, but I come right back. Then she makes tiny warning gestures at Um Zaki, but these only make her tell even bawdier stories and make me want to stay even more.

My mother tries to scold her by asking, "When will you fast and pray?"

"For the whole month before Doomsday!" is always her answer.

She's a widow of fifty, a well of jokes and zest and laughter. Her son Zaki is a carpenter in our alley. He walks with his head held high, for though his mother is hilarious, she never does anything to be ashamed of. True, she's a bit addicted to cigarettes, coffee, and the records of Munira Al-Mahdaya, but she has a close friend in every household. She's never been part of a single quarrel, a remarkable feat in an alley loaded with strife.

* * * * *

One day my mother sighs and says, "You poor dear, Um Zaki, may Allah watch over you and heal you."

She is really very ill and steadily gets worse. She loses weight with incredible speed, like a ball being deflated, and her frame hangs with folds of empty skin. The eternal wisdom of our alley pronounces her disease "totally unknown," says it must have been caused by the jinn, and decides she'll never recover unless she holds a rite of exorcism.

The heralded day of the zar arrives. Our neighbor's house is packed to bursting with women. The smell of incense is everywhere. A troop of mysterious Sudanese women dominate the house with shadowy secrets. I peek through the skylight and see my friend in a new scene. In a robe gaudy with sequins and bangles, she sits on a throne. An ivory crown dangling with beads of every color perches on her head, and her legs soak in a deep basin of rosewater with green coffee beans in the bottom. The women thump huge tambourines, their brassy throats cast out shivering songs. The breath of demons fills the air, and each demon grabs a guest for a dancing partner. The room shimmers with their gyrations and vibrates with their wailing moans as human and ghost melt together. In the middle of it all, Um Zaki writhes wildly as if caught again by the mad frenzies of youth. She wheezes sharply through her golden teeth, then begins to run around the throne. But her run becomes a frightening rush, round and round, whirling faster and faster until she starts to wobble in exhaustion and falls at last unconscious . . .

A shrill trilling of joy rattles the room, and one exultant, ecstatic voice resounds above it: "O Seal of the Prophets, witness us!"

* * * * *

14

And the days pass.

And the health of our friend does not improve.

She doesn't joke now. She doesn't laugh. She wonders fearfully, "Um Zaki, where are you? What has happened to you? What has happened to me, oh Lord?"

Her son is finally forced to send her to a government hospital. She leaves in a jolting donkey cart, and my wet eyes bid her farewell. She sees me standing there and waves to me, saying, "Pray for me. Allah listens to children."

So I raise my face to the sky and murmur, "Oh, Lord, bring Auntie back to us."

But it was as if the donkey cart had taken her to the Land of Waka-Waka.

3

The day is lovely but redolent with mystery.

My father watches me thoughtfully, smiles at me gently while sipping coffee, tousles my hair, and pats my shoulder on his way out of the house.

And as she does her housework, my mother is nervous. She ignores my monkeyshines and even encourages me. "Have fun, honey."

No scowls, no scoldings, no threats.

I go up to the roof for a while and come down to find our Syrian neighbor Um Barhum. I run into the kitchen to tell my mother, but she's not there. I keep calling for her till Um Barhum says, "Your mommy is running an errand. I'm staying with you till she gets back."

"But I want to go out and play!"

"What? And leave me here alone—your guest?"

So I have to put up with it.

A knock at the door. Um Barhum, gesturing for me to sit still, opens it herself. In come Am Hassan, the barber, and his apprentice, both smiling. When I see them, I say, "My father is out."

The old man answers, "We're your guests! Besides, we're going to teach you an unusual game." He sits on the sofa and recites the invocation: "In the name of Allah, the Compassionate, the Merciful!" Then, while taking some bright shiny instruments from his bag, he says: "Wouldn't you like to know how to use these things?"

To hide my confusion, I run over to him.

The apprentice makes me sit on a stool in front of his master and explains, "This is the best way."

All of a sudden, he grabs me deftly and clutches my arms and legs; his fierce arms are nailed and glued to me. I yell in outrage, "Let go of me!" I beg Um Barhum for help, but she is gone like a dissolved speck of salt . . .

All is a blur until the terrible operation begins, a cruel, monstrous assault I can neither escape nor prevent, only undergo helplessly. Oh, how the barbed claws of intense pain gouge my flesh! With demonic cunning, it flows from the surface of my body to its core. Oh, how my screeches smash walls and pierce every corner of the alley!

*   *   *   *   *

Everything is blurred again for some time. I sink deep into a watery world between waking and sleeping. Prismatic eons of terror and sorrow wash over me. At last my mother's face appears above me, heavy with apology and encouragement. Before I can open my mouth to protest or accuse, she fills my hands with candy.

For several days, I live between memories of agony and heaps of festive sweets. The house overflows with friends. I walk around with my legs apart and hold my gallabiya away from my body.

4

I'm on my way to the arch when the flour merchant's door opens and his three daughters come out. Light beams from them and dazzles sight and soul. Their light hair, blue eyes, and unveiled faces glow with pure beauty. A horse cart is waiting for them, but I stand between it and the girls, nailed to the spot. They notice my captivation, and the one in the middle, the plumpest and most lush-lipped, says, "What's with this guy, blocking our way?"

I still don't budge, so she exclaims mischievously, "Hey, you, wake up!"

Engulfed by the flood of life in all its obscurity, I reply, "My nightingale, *khoon deli khord wakuli hasel kared.*"

They burst out laughing, and the oldest girl says, "He must be a dervish."

The middle one adds, "He must be crazy."

I fling myself into archway darkness and stagger around until I reach the light of the takiya square. My head buzzes and my heart whispers like the ecstasy of buds before blooming.

Their ravishing portaits hang deep in my deepest gallery.

Seeds of love planted too early to grow.

5

It's a happy day.

I'm going with my mother to visit the wife of our local police prefect.

It pours down rain all morning, but it's nice again by noon, the sun shining. Water bulges the cheeks of the road and fills its hollows, but I'm happy to be on the way to the prefect's wife.

She is an enormous woman, extremely dark, with a tattoo in the dimple of her chin. Her laughter is piercing and her voice carries a strange village lilt. Her cat has thick fur of the purest white and purrs constantly like a Sufi telling prayer beads.

She hugs my mother in welcome while I wait, then turns to me with a laugh and messes up my hair. She lifts me high into the air, then crushes me to her breast. I sink into deep softness and feel her great paunch, a lush mattress which floods my being with warmth.

I follow her while trying to rearrange my disheveled hair and clothes, not yet recovered from that gust of warmth.

She says to my mother, "I'm sure there are demons living in that vaulted archway."

My mother piously invokes Allah, and the giantess continues, "They come out just after midnight."

My mother warns her not to look out the window at that time.

I play with the cat until it disappears under the sofa. Stuck on the wall above two crossed swords is a bull's head; I stare at it and wish I could reach it. I yearn for the warm hug at the end of the visit.

The conversation continues, meandering everywhere.

She lights the gaslamp hanging from the ceiling.

A moth flits around the light.

I wonder: will it ever come, the moment of leave-taking with its promise of warmth?

6

In mosque school, boys and girls sit together on the same mat and recite the verses in one voice. The leather lash of our teacher the sheikh doesn't see any difference between a boy's shin and a girl's. We all sit cross-legged for lunch, faces to the wall; each unknots his bundle and spreads it out. Everybody has a flat round bread, cheese, and some helwa.

I steal glimpses of Darwisha while she recites or eats.

I follow her down the street till she turns into her dead-end lane. Then I go on to my house, carrying my slate and her image.

When the proper time for it comes, we visit the cemetery, and I get left sitting in the courtyard at the entrance. Bored, I run out into the grounds. There, by accident, we meet, Darwisha and I, among the roof-less tombs of the poor.

I give her half my pastry, and we exchange glances as we eat.

"Where do you play?"

"In the lane."

Though her lane branches off our street, I don't dare sneak into it in broad daylight. The feeling that stops me is unclear, but I know it isn't innocent. We now make silent promises with our eyes. When evening comes, I go into her lane and find her standing on her doorstep.

We stand there, two silent phantoms shrouded in darkness and guilt.

"Shouldn't we sit down?"

She doesn't answer.

I sit on the step and tug at her hand to make her join me, then slide over till we are side by side. A strange and mysterious joy flows over me. Taking her chin in my hand, I turn her face to mine, lean toward her and kiss her. I put my arm around her. I am silent, spellbound, melting into a mist of rushing sensations; I know drunkenness before touching liquor.

We forget time and fear.

We forget our families and the alley.

Even the phantoms cannot part us.

On hot summer nights we spread mats and cushions out on the roof and stay up very late, our light the light of the stars or the moon. The cats cavort among us, and the clucking of our chickens keeps us company. Sometimes the wife and three daughters of our Syrian neighbor, Hag Bisheer, join us. They enjoy singing their mountain songs, and I listen with a thirst almost as strong as my craving for light skin and blue eyes.

The mother and daughters, the oldest of whom is ten, bewitch me, and I insist on being allowed to listen. The music makes me light, and I join in and sing so well our neighbor says, "What a lovely voice you have, my boy!"

So, in this society of the night, I get a chance to show off my talent while my small heart revels in feminine beauty. Singing becomes my hobby, and Munira Al-Mahdaya, the popular singer, becomes the apple of my eye. But I sing those mountain songs not only with my voice but with my heart.

One day our neighbor says to my mother, "The boy does have a beautiful voice."

My mother answers proudly, "Really?"

"It would be a shame to neglect it."

"Let him sing all he wants to; it beats goofing off."

"Wouldn't you like your son to be a singer?"

My mother is too shocked to answer, so our neighbor goes on. "What's wrong with Mr. Anwar and Mr. Abdul Lateef?"

"I dream he'll become a government official like his father and brothers—"

"—Oh, but a singer makes much more money!"

I listen carefully as I sit on our neighbor's lap, enchanted by warmth and glory.

* * * * *

The music and happiness don't last long. One day I see my mother shaking her head sadly and mumbling, "What a shame."

I ask her why she's unhappy. "Our nice neighbors are going back to Syria."

My heart aches even though I don't grasp the extent of the loss. "Is it far?"

She answers sadly, "Farther than we can reach."

With all my heart I want to change reality, to turn time backward to yesterday, but how?

When they are ready to leave in the carriage, I bid them a final farewell, kissing the hand of Hag Bisheer. I watch the carriage until it disappears around the corner into the brass district. I cry for a long time and taste the bitterness of separation, gloom, and an empty world.

8

Festivals at the cemetery give me great delight.

The night before our visit, we fix dates and pastry. Early in the morning, carrying reed mats and some sweet basil, I walk between my parents, and the servants go before us with mercy-baskets full of food.

The scurrying current of carts and people makes me happy. The gate of the cemetery is an old friend, and our family vault, with its austere dignity, towering tombstones, and hidden secrets, appeals to me. My father's attitude toward it strikes me as odd, but my own attraction to it is no different from my fascination with a little cactus nearby. Under the sky's full arc, I break into leaps of joy and bursts of exploration nothing can dampen. When I see the blind reciter and the beggars, fawning like dogs for the mercy-offerings, my happiness is complete.

But the picture changes when Hemam enters.

My sister and her son come to stay with us. Hemam is about fourteen, a charming, lively companion who banishes loneliness. A blithe and gentle spirit, he plays with me with never a hint of boredom, believing my innocent fibs and fantasies.

One day I find him lying silent. When I ask him to play, he doesn't answer. They tell me he is sick . . .

Thick folds of anxiety hang heavy in the dreary, tormented air. Dark feelings come to me, and when I see my mother's deep worry and my sister's fear, my sadness grows. Then Hemam's father comes . . .

I want to know what's happening, but they shove me aside and say, "None of your business. Go out and play."

But I know it's something out of the ordinary . . .

And so serious my mother cries. My sister shrieks. From far away, I glimpse my friend on the bed, wrapped up like a pillow, with not a chink left to breathe through. The word "death" is repeated all around me. I see that it's a parting without end so I cry with the mourners, and my heart suffers more than its age can bear.

Visits to the tomb lose their delight. The sight of the place makes me wonder what lies beneath the tomb, and its silence depresses me. I don't feel better when they tell me Hemam is having a good time watering the gardens of Paradise. The pain of parting fails to fade with passing days. There is nothing but sorrow and lost love and fear and cruel memory and the heavy weight of the mysterious unknown.

9

At home and in the alley, you hear the gossip over and over.

A neighbor asks my mother, "Hey, by the way, did you hear the strange news?" My mother begs her to go on. "About Tawheeda, daughter of Um Ali and Am Ragab."

"What about her, for heaven's sake?"

"She's gone to work for the government."

"Gone to work for the government?"

"I swear it's true. A government official—she goes to the ministry and mixes with men!"

"God be our refuge and strength! But her family's so decent, her mother's so nice, her father's a real man—"

"—Words, words, words. Would a real man put up with this?"

"Oh Lord, our God, protect us now and in the last days."

"Well, the poor girl's no beauty. Maybe that's why."

"She'd have got herself a husband sooner or later—but not now, of course."

Ceaseless alley tongues babble her story, make fun of her, and criticize her. I take it all in. Whenever her father appears, someone is sure to say, "God preserve us" and "What are men coming to?"

Tawheeda is the first woman from our part of town to work for the government. My family chatters on about how she and my sister were classmates in mosque school. Because of what I hear, I stand at the entrance to the alley and wait to see her climb down from the donkey cart on her way home from work. Intent, I watch her approach, face unveiled, an exhausted look in her eyes. She walks briskly, like no other woman or girl in our alley. Maybe she glances at me, maybe she doesn't even see me, and then she's gone.

And I mutter like a parrot, "What are men coming to?"

10

Um Abdu is the best-known woman in our alley.

She's as strong as a mule and as insolent as a gangster. Even her burly cart-driver husband backs off when faced with her feisty temper.

She has two beautiful daughters, Dawlet and Ahsan.

The whole neighborhood—the shopkeeper, laborer, peddler, bum—maintains a fond, friendly relation to her. In every house, she finds a job that pays, serving as go-between, mediator, matchmaker. At weddings, she's the mashta, making up the bride's face and depilating her body. If you want to buy something, you go to Um Abdu; in her dallala role, she's sure to know who has that very item for sale. And when there's a really serious feud, the family she sides with usually wins because of her whiplash tongue—*and* her knowledge of everybody's secrets.

Sometimes she visits my mother and talks about her adventures. When she acts out the latest quarrel, her voice gets louder, rises in pitch, trembles with anger and outrage and personal slander. You begin to think her act is a real fight.

On feast days she's quite courteous, taking us in her cart to visit the Al-Magawri mosque and Abu Saud, the famous healer.

When we need her, I get to go to her house. I hurry with a light heart, longing to see the donkey tied to a stake in her yard, eager to be with Dawlet and Ahsan.

Dawlet is a good girl, able to make out printed words, and she knows a few chapters of the Koran by heart. An educated young man from the quarter falls in love with her. He overlooks the social gap, risks being a relative of Um Abdu, and marries her.

Ahsan's character is her mother's in miniature—except that *she* is dazzlingly beautiful. Stamped in the same mold as Um Abdu, she's so willful, violent, and sassy she often defies her awesome mother. Exciting battles break out between them. One hard-working young man after another courts her, but she rejects them all in the hope of a match as extraordinary as her sister's.

Despite the difference in our ages, I'm her friend. In my eyes, vague desires mingle with veiled signals sent out by instincts I don't even know I have. Her vast, rich, bubbling, bouncing body overwhelms me. Once in a while, she lets me help her do the laundry in the courtyard. As I carry the tin washbucket by its wooden handle, I sway with its weight. I sit across from her and take the clothes after she's wrung them out. While I'm stacking them in the tub, my eyes sneak up her dress; she watches me out of the corner of her eye with a neutral smile.

"Here," she says one day. "Take this handkerchief of mine to Sheikh Labeeb."

He's in his usual place facing the archway. He squats on a fur and wears a white skullcap, an embroidered gallabiya, and kohl on his eyelids. Over his nose, his brows make a deep V. I give him the handkerchief, one millieme, and a lump of sugar. He smells the handkerchief, thinks a while, then says, "Very soon your hope chest will fill and the bird will sing."

I go back to Ahsan saying the words over and over to remember them, happy as usual to do anything to serve her.

And the owner of a business renting large tents for weddings and funerals asks for her hand. He's a rich man, about fifty, with a wife and children, and she marries him. But after a couple of years, she disappears completely from his house and the quarter, leaving behind an uproar of rumor, terrible disgrace, and a scar on the pride of Um Abdu.

*   *   *   *   *

Then on one among many nights of careening, unstoppable time, I find myself face to face with Ahsan. She dances and sings that cheap song with the line "Swim in the water, Oh Syrian daughter."

She sees me and the light of recognition streams from her eyes. I'm in a stupor, but she comes up to me with a simple smile of reassurance, takes me by the hand, and leads me to her room. Then she locks the door and bursts out laughing. "The world is large," she says, "but only a pinhole after all."

As I peer into her face, she asks about her mother.

"She's just fine."

"And Dawlet?"

"Her oldest boy is in school."

"And your mother and sisters?"

"Very well."

She says warmly, "Come see me often."

I hesitate, then ask, "How did you get here?"

She laughs and says sarcastically, "The same way you did!"

11

We've finished mosque school and have taken the primary school entrance exam. Now, in small clusters, we stand in the courtyard and wait for our results.

24

An official comes out of the principal's office and reads a list of names, then says: "If you heard your name, stay here. If not, go home."

I didn't hear my name. Joy drenches me since I figure my failure means no more education, no more teacher's lash. Life will be soft and carefree from now on.

When my father asks how I came out, I answer blithely, "Oh, I failed and came home . . ."

"Ycchs . . . I thought you were better than that."

"It's not important," I say gaily.

"Not important?"

"I hate mosque school and I hate our master the sheikh and I hate the lessons, so thank God I'm done with all that stuff."

He knits his brow in wonder, "You think you're going to stay home?"

"Sure, that'll be much better."

"And play with the scum of the alley, is that the idea?"

As I look at him uneasily, his stern voice commands, "You'll go back to mosque school for another year so the whip can treat your idiocy."

I start to object, but he says, "Prepare for a long life of learning. You shall learn step by step until you become a civilized human being."

So I only enjoyed the happiness of failure for a couple of hours.

12

What is happening to the world?

Floods sweep over it, earthquakes shake it, fire burns its skirts, slogans explode from its throat.

Thousands—more than ever before—burst the great square, and their screams as they threaten with clenched fists rattle the walls of our alley and deafen our ears. Now even women ride in the rows of carts and take part in the frenzy . . .

Over the wall along our roof, I watch and ask myself what is happening to the world . . .

Speeches, electric and passionate, smash through the air and pour down a deluge of new words: Saad Zaghloul, Malta, the Sultan, the Crescent and the Cross, the Nation, sudden death . . .

Flags wave above shops, posters of Saad Zaghloul plaster walls, the imam of the mosque appears in the minaret to call and preach. And I tell myself that what is happening is strange but exciting and entertaining, truly magnificent.

Except that I witness a chase.

People rush into our street, throw rocks, and flatten themselves against our alley walls for protection.

Horsemen with tall hats and thick mustaches crash down the alley. Fierce, frightful voices ring out, then screams. Someone yanks me away from my lookout and pushes me into the house where terrified faces peer out at me and say, "It is death."

We strain our ears behind closed shutters but hear only voices in strife, footsteps, neighs, the buzz of bullets, a scream of agony, raging chants.

This lasts several minutes, then silence falls on the alley.

The uproar starts again, now at a distance . . . then total silence.

And I tell myself that what is happening is strange and terrifying and dreadful.

I know only a little about the new words Saad Zaghloul, Malta, the Sultan, and the Nation, but I know a lot about the British cavalry, bullets, and death.

Um Abdu, extremely wrought up, comes to tell tales of heroes and martyrs. She eulogizes Ilwa the baker's apprentice and swears the soldiers' horses became headstrong and uncomfortable in front of the takiya and threw their riders to the ground . . .

And I tell myself that what is happening is an exciting and unbelievable dream.

13

This short, polite, intelligent boy, just at the dawn of young manhood, is, I am told, my cousin Sabry.

I don't know his father—my father's brother—very well, for he seldom leaves the countryside; in fact, Sabry is seeing Cairo for the first time. I gather from conversations overheard at night that my uncle is putting him in high school in Cairo because the authorities suspected he'd been involved in revolutionary activities back in his home town.

With a fascinated look, I ask him if he goes to demonstrations and shouts "Long live Saad!"

He smiles without answering. He seems deeper than his age.

My father tells him, "Our house is your house. You're safe here, but you have to be careful."

I pipe up with, "But Daddy, you went on strike with the government officials yourself."

"And why don't you mind your own business?"

Sabry is a diligent student with a great appetite for work.

But one evening, faint worry clouds his clever eyes, so I ask what's bothering him. "What makes you think anything's bothering me?" he says warily.

"You're just not your usual self."

He invites me for a walk through the alley. We stroll till nightfall and hang around the judge's house. Then he whispers in my ear: "I guess you'd be able to hand out papers to some people, wouldn't you?"

"Yes, but why should I"

"Okay, so forget it if it bothers you."

Glad to be trusted with a task, no matter what, I agree. So I go along handing papers to shopkeepers and passers-by. They take them with surprise, glance at them, smile, and then go on about their business.

I return to Sabry at the head of the alley. "Happy?" he asks.

I express boundless joy, and he warns me, "Don't you dare tell my uncle or aunt."

And it's a long time before I find out I was distributing political pamphlets.

14

This day starts with a mocking demonstration. It's amazing how people fool around in the brief periods between bloody encounters. It's coming, a huge demonstration led by a donkey draped in white cloth painted with red letters that say "Sultan Fo'ad," for the Sultan has just betrayed the Nation.

One of our native sons, sporting a British helmet, rides the donkey through an ever-growing roar:

Yah, Fo'ad, you crummy louse-face!
Who told you to turn about face?

This taunt is met with shouts and shrill trilling-cries.

I take my father a piece of local news that has enflamed my imagination: "They say eggs are coming out of chickens with Saad's name on them."

My father and a visitor laugh. The guest says, "Saad's enemies try never to look into his eyes while arguing because of the piercing rays that shoot out."

This enchants my father, who murmurs, "Heaven's gift to us."

The guest cries, "The years of disaster are over and the days of happiness [saad] with Saad are going to begin!"

My father sighs. "I feel so sorry for the man, the sheikh, sick and in exile.

"Saad sick? How can that be, Daddy?" Nobody pays any attention to me. I insist: "Saad cannot possibly be sick." Then I get adamant. "Next you'll be telling me he will die like my nephew Hemam."

15

A group of friends comes to see my father and talk about the revolution. Nobody talks about anything else these days. Revolutionary language even punctuates our childish prattle, and we base our games on demonstrations and slogans. English patrols are now a common sight. We stare at their handsome faces in wonder, puzzled by the contrast between their atrocities and their elegance.

The conversation goes round and round.

"Who can believe all this? Even part of it is too much!"

"It is Allah, the Compassionate, the Merciful."

"He can raise the dead to life!"

"Fellaheen, workers, students, officials, and even women are killing and being killed."

"The fellah bears arms and defies the Empire."

"The complete disruption of transport has cut Egypt into several small nations."

"Ah, and the butchery?"

"The massacre of Al-Azhar."

"The massacre of Asyut."

"Al-Azeeza. Al-Badrasheen."

"Hosaynayah."

"I'm not me and you're not you—Long live Saad!"

"Yes, by Allah, long live the great magician!"

"But the dead are beyond count."

"They live with Allah."

One man starts telling the legend of Saad as he has heard it, concentrating on his encounters with the British and the khedive before the revolution.

And I see my father's eyes fill with tears.

Amazed, I watch him, flushed with silent excitement, and a flood of tears streams down my cheeks.

The first martyr from our neighborhood is Salooma. Ilwa the baker's apprentice was killed here, true, but he actually came from Kafr Izzagari. Salooma's father, Am Tulba, roams around peddling cotton candy from a cart. Salooma would help out, falling asleep on the front of the pushcart when he got tired.

When a demonstration passes through the wide courtyard in front of the judge's house, Salooma joins in automatically; his father doesn't notice. In the Gafer district, the English pounce on the demonstration and open fire. A bullet hits Salooma in the head and he drops down dead.

As the news spreads through the alley, grief floods it, and it trembles with admiration and pride. People come to console Am Tulba and sprinkle his hands with pearls of words. In spite of his grief and exhaustion, he is swept away by an emotion he's never felt before: for the first time in his life, he finds himself in the midst of citizens of every class, respected by people who never bothered to return his greetings before. Rich merchants and employers shower him with gifts and money.

Salooma's funeral is the greatest the neighborhood has ever seen. Every other funeral, even those of gangster leaders, notables, and religious people, shrinks in comparison. The men walk behind the flag-draped coffin, and the woman hail it from roofs and windows. Since hundreds from nearby districts join the cortege, it reaches the Hussein Mosque with all the glory of a full-strength demonstration.

Conversations now center on the funeral, Salooma fades to name and symbol, the bereaved and struggling father attains a prominent position, and alley commentators speak of the wonder of life which changes values in an instant among instants of magic.

17

One morning I wake up to find a woman and a young girl in the house.

"Come and meet your aunt and her daughter So'ad," says my mother.

I greet them with the shyness natural to first meetings. The woman looks a bit like my father and the girl is extremely beautiful.

My aunt asks, "What year are you in, honey?"

"Second grade."

I am smitten with love for the girl, who fills me with pleasant magic and bright dreams.

Then I find out my aunt has come from Minya because her daughter, who will soon be married, needs things for her new apartment. My aunt spends her short time in Cairo visiting furniture shops, upholsterers, and carpenters with my father.

In her free time, So'ad appears in elegant dresses and charming make-up, glowing with the colors of brides, fragrant with their aroma. With devoted heart and obscure longing, I glance furtively at her.

She looks through the shutters and remarks, "This street of yours is very entertaining."

"Come on, come with me and I'll show you all the little lanes and the archway and the takiya of the Sufis."

But she ignores my invitation. My glance glides along her neck, grabs glimpses of her legs. I yearn for an obscure fusion, some vague gratification, some experience unknown, and I want to touch her rosy cheek. I refuse to believe that in a few days she'll leave my heart with no one to keep it company.

I pluck up enough courage to say, "You know what?"

Then voice and brain stop.

She encourages me to go on. "Know what?"

I'm still tongue-tied, so she asks, "Why are you looking at me like that?"

"Who? Me?"

"Yes. I've seen you. Don't deny it." She laughs a short laugh. "You're a naughty boy."

And my heart contracts with guilt.

*   *   *   *   *

My mother and my aunt take turns looking at a picture of So'ad. My aunt says, "The groom insists on seeing a photograph."

"And your husband agreed?"

"I guess so. Sort of."

My father's voice booms from his room: "Improper behavior."

"Well, times are changing," says my mother.

"It's only a picture," my aunt says, "and the groom is a real find from an excellent family."

In a tone not at all free of protest, my father says, "As Allah wills."

I follow this with concealed sorrow. A warning of endless separation lurks in its undertones, and I see the face of sadness on the horizon.

The days of the visit pass incredibly fast and I can do nothing to stop them.

The moment of parting arrives.

I gaze at So'ad's rosy cheek, a loaf of fresh bread from the oven, and then they go away, just like the Basheer family before.

My mother teases me about my sadness without realizing the depth of my suffering.

18

Joy dances in every heart, ecstasy burns every soul: it is the day of Saad's return from exile.

My father comes home as if from a brawl. His tarboosh has lost its tassle, the knot of his tie is crammed up under his collar, his jacket is dyed by dust and sweat, and he's as hoarse as if he'd been coughing for ages, but his eyes shine with victorious light. He throws himself into the sofa and says: "I cheered till I lost my voice. Just completely forgot myself."

With deep satisfaction, he adds, "The whole world was there in Sayeeda Square. Praise to Thee, oh Lord, nothing outnumbers Thy worshippers!"

The neighborhood is swept by a great feeling of triumph; every heart believes freedom is knocking at the door. Huge demonstrations in the district go on and on. Saad . . . Saad . . . Long live Saad! I get caught up in the cheering fever and am sorry the demonstrators don't come into our alley because it's almost a dead end; there's no outlet at one side except the narrow path along the takiya that empties into the cemetery.

When I ask my mother if the British will leave, she answers with fierce conviction, "Never to return!"

That night we celebrate the end of our leader's exile with a big festival. Lights deck shop fronts, flags fly, trilling-cries ring out, and the alma Al-Mazayyah volunteers to brighten the night. A platform ringed by her orchestra is put up in the middle of the market, chairs are lined up in front of it, and to the music of the oud, kanoon, riq, and nay, the men dance and she sings:

Nights of pleasure now rejoin our nights.

And, punning on Saad's last name and our expensive, hybrid dates:

Oh Zaghloul dates, you are the sweetest.

She ends with a jokey new song that begins:

Allenby, you brat, what happened, you son of a shrew?
Our freedom has come in spite of Great Britain and you.

The booza overflows with drunks, the ghurzas glow with fiery heaps of hot hashish on coals, and even the idiots and bums and thieves stay up late and have a good time.

Am Tulba, father of our local martyr, comes to the party, and even Sheikh Labeeb attends.

I stay awake for a long time at my window, and a mysterious power charges my small heart with magic vitality.

19

My father peers at me strangely and asks what I've been up to. I respond with joy and pride, "I joined the big demonstration."

"You could have been trampled to death."

"Lots of kids took part."

He stifles a grin and questions me in an examiner's tone. "Now that Saad Zaghloul has come home from exile and become prime minister, what's the point in demonstrating?"

"To support him in his stand against the king."

"Who says?"

"The students' leader says Saad has resigned to protest the king's stand on the constitution. We must support our leader."

"And just what, exactly, is the bone of contention between Saad and the king?"

I stop blathering in perplexity and my father laughs, but then I surprise him: "We are with Saad and against the king."

"Great. And what did you chant today in Aabadeen Square?"

" 'Saad or Revolution!' "

"Which means?"

I think for a while and say, "The meaning is clear: Saad or Revolution."

He smiles. "Marvelous. Who won?"

"Saad. And we shouted, 'Long live the king!' and 'Hail Saad!' " I go on, getting excited again. "Taking part in demonstrations is the most enjoyable thing in the world."

"As long as the British don't participate," my father says with a smile.

20

Yehya Mudkoor is my best friend and the best soccer player in our school.

One day I find him reading a book at recess. "What's that?"

"*Johnson's Son,* the first episode of a new detective serial."

He lends me the book when he finishes it, and I read it with a joy never experienced before. I finish that serial and go on to another and then another until I end up addicted to books.

In time I become the star of stars in reading. As for my friend, he soon gives it up to settle on the throne of soccer.

21

My memory always links Ibrahim Tawfeek with clowning and taking dares. He's the congenial, half-crazy star of schoolyard pebble soccer. From a heap of rubble behind the ancient fountain, we pick out a walnut-sized stone for a ball and play a match every day in the long recess after lunch. This is officially forbidden, but the staff usually looks the other way during lunch unless the headmaster turns up, and then the game stops abruptly. So, completely without supervision, we play a rough game indeed, devastating our shoes, and parents must pay the price!

During the short recess, Ibrahim Tawfeek squashes his tarboosh down till it looks like a skullcap, turns his jacket around backwards, and imitates Charlie Chaplin, walking back and forth while we clap in rhythm. To conclude his act, he recites the monologue:

> Oh you who were left uncle-less,
> Utterly bereft and nickle-less,
> I stood by you in times of fickleness.

One day he's boasting about the tricks he pulls on his stepfather when someone pipes up, "Hey, I dare you to eat a hot hornpepper."

This is just the sort of challenge that obliges him to attempt the impossible, so he shouts, "I can eat ten!"

Two sides form and start betting each other. We buy ten hot hornpeppers from the stewbean peddler and eagerly gather around Ibrahim.

He chews the first horn with fake nonchalance.

He keeps his poise and unconcern intact during the second.

The third doesn't change the way he looks, but he swallows his saliva quite palpably.

After the fourth goes down, he hacks out a stifled cough.

The fifth makes his eyes water in spite of his mighty self-control, and he coughs rather violently.

While the sixth is in his mouth, he appears to be fighting an unseen foe in his very depths, and tears pour from his eyes.

When he downs number seven, water streams from his nose—now a very deep red.

A few tender hearts cry out, "Call off the bet."

With but a slight movement of his head, as if he can't speak, Ibrahim refuses.

Water from his eyes joins water from his nose in a canal that soaks his chin and throat. Cough spasms rack him.

His lips swell and his face turns purple, but, to cheers and applause, he swallows every last hornpepper. So he wins . . .

But he doesn't seem to feel the joy of victory. He stands silent and red and glazed. Such is the situation when we walk into religion class.

The sheikh is always after him because he's notorious for negligence and mischief. "Ibrahim Tawfeek, recite the sura beginning 'Blessed is the One . . .'"

Ibrahim, drowned in his hidden problem, says nothing.

"Stand up, boy, and recite!"

When Ibrahim fails to rise, whispers start to seep out of the corners of the room, and the sheikh thinks it's all a planned prank. He screams, "Courtesy, you sons of dogs! Stand up, you brat! Stand up! Let there be no blessing from God on you or those who got you!"

When the sheikh gets near Ibrahim's place in the back of the classroom, he's flabbergasted at the way his face looks. He stands there and says, bewildered, "What's wrong with you? Why are you crying?"

We all start to speak up for Ibrahim. The sheikh listens with amazement and shouts, "Allah forbid . . . you sons of devils! You're all evildoers and the sons of evildoers . . ."

And Ibrahim goes off to the dispensary for treatment.

But he never gives up clowning and taking dares.

Hasham Zayid and I sit on the same bench.

Though he's a tall, husky, muscular boy, he's also kind, shy, and well-behaved. Because his mother owns several houses in Birma Street and half of the biggest spice business in the district, we both admire and envy Hasham. When Ibrahim Tawfeek's jokes sneak up behind him, he can't stifle his laughter. The teacher sees him instead of the real culprit, so he gets the punishment—slap, kick, or punch—and takes it like the polite, submissive student he is.

Hasham flunks out of school but becomes, when his mother dies, one of the most influential men in the alley. Our paths separate. Once in a while I see him in a carriage or, wearing native dress, enthroned in a halo of sycophants. His personality becomes weird, so I avoid even shaking hands with him. He swaggers, puts on airs, and aggressively exploits his power to impose his will on people. How could a shy, kind boy change into this ferocious monster? I ponder and wonder in vain . . .

Not a day of his life goes by without a fight, for he thinks wallops are quicker than words. He prefers clubs to fists. When he takes over the square, we all avoid him like the plague.

Had he lived during the gangster period, he'd have been a futuwa, a gang leader. Since he didn't, he's nothing but a neighborhood pest and a headache for the police. He spends a lot of time in jail but gets out by bribing the officers and the sheikh of the alley.

Though always surrounded by his court, he doesn't have a single friend, and in spite of his wealth, he never marries nor is known to care about women.

His attitude to the memory of his mother is puzzling and thought-provoking, for he sometimes recalls her with deep sorrow and prays for mercy on her soul but at other times criticizes her with bitter sarcasm and says things like, "She was niggardly and greedy, neglected herself to the point of filthiness, and treated our servants with insane severity . . ."

One day he overdoes his attack on her and then suddenly breaks into tears, forgetting himself completely. When he realizes he's behaving like a weakling, he laughs—but later vents his rage on everyone who saw him cry and holds a grudge against them . . .

And Hasham Zayid vanishes from the alley and from his house.

He's missing for such a long time he begins to melt into murky oblivion.

You hear people say he has emigrated and you hear people whisper he has been murdered, his body hidden.

One morning I am awakened with sudden harshness. A dark grip grabs and jerks me from the land of dreams. A flood of jangling noise engulfs me. My hair stands on end with horror: voices wail in the hall. Terrible thoughts rip at my flesh and the spector of death rises up before my eyes.

I jump out of bed and dash to my closed door, hesitate a moment, then throw it open to face the unknown.

My father is seated, my mother leans against the sideboard, and the servant stands in the doorway. They are all crying.

My mother sees me and comes to me. "We scared you . . . Don't be afraid, son."

Through a dry throat, I ask, "What . . .?"

She whispers hoarsely in my ear, "Saad Zaghloul . . . May he live on in you!"

I cry from my soul, "Saad!"

I go back to my room.

Gloom hangs everywhere.

24

Nipples engorged and swollen, the cat lies on her side while the little ones blindly jostle each other in her bosom. Alone in the room, I study this scene closely. All of a sudden, I hear breathing and look around. It's Senaya, our postman's oldest daughter, some years older than I. Her fine features and feathery spirit brim over with vitality and joy. Entranced, she gazes at the cat and whispers, "Nothing could be more beautiful."

When I answer with a nod, she says, "I love cats, don't you?"

Unable to think of anything but how close we are, I say, "Yes, I . . ."

Then she presses even closer to see better and I feel her breasts against my shoulder. She goes on talking but I don't hear her. I'm on fire, the flames lick up my shyness, and I spin around and crush her to my chest. And so begins a close relationship filled, on my side, with both joy and regret.

I come to know her better, beautiful and bold as she is wary. Though she becomes wonderfully, melodiously drunk with passion, there are still uncrossable barriers between us. I obey her signals, rush into her shelter—but she doesn't understand innocence or dreams or even secret conspiracies and so lures me into the rose garden where she kindles all the fires of hell. We know neither peace nor safety and pluck buds while we tremble in fear of the guardians. We run in a fever of love, two madly snatching pickpockets hovering between conflict and open-eyed drowsiness. Life is a crazy song overflowing with sweetness and pain.

After two years of our love, Senaya gets married.

We meet again years and years later.

She has grown stupendously fat and has a sleepy look, but she's sensible, too, very dignified, balanced, and stable. We shake hands and hold an ordinary gossipy conversation without one meaningful smile, remark, or gesture. She's a respectable lady, a living symbol of mother-hood, devotion, and piety.

I flash back to the time of her ripening youth when she was a butter-fly of many hues, a fresh apple, a sweet flower, a flowing stream.

Those were happy days.

25

Senaya's sister Fathaya is just my age, an image of sweet comfort and calm depth.

We sneak shy glances that stir fascinating hopes. I touch her arm, but she gently pushes my hand away and says gracefully, "I don't care for fooling around."

Tired of her seriousness, I say, "You don't understand love."

"You're the one who doesn't understand," she sadly responds, and reproaches me with, "Prove you know love the way I do."

Tears trace my cheeks like hot candle wax and despair clutches me, so I decide to cure myself by giving her up. I go away resolved to forget her, but desire, a chance meeting, or a wistful message draws me back to face her loving heart, pure feeling, and unyielding will.

I have chosen a path too long and difficult to allow early marriage, so my girl is wooed by many suitors. Her father tells her, "Keep on re-fusing like this and you'll wait forever."

He finally puts his foot down. "Look, hearts change in ten days. You'll get over it and be very happy." And he marries her off to a nice respectable man. She marries him with a broken heart, has children, keeps house, and is thought to have a happy and successful marriage.

She disappears from my sight and fantasies for a long time.

I meet her at a funeral when she is about sixty, ten years a widow. As we shake hands, she gazes at me with a look aglow with the bright smile of old memory. Something hidden deep inside is moved. A wave of nostalgia and sadness sweeps over me, and the weight of time stretched out behind us crushes me down.

Her daughters are all married, I discover, and she lives alone with an old servant. In spite of everything, I find myself talking to her quite boldly because so little is left of our lives. I even decide to visit her.

While I imagine this, both bitterness and joy draw me toward her, but then I meekly submit to the sorrow of farewell.

26

Sitt Nagayah is a lonely woman.

I remember her as alone, always, all by herself in her house, her name said without a surname like a limb ripped from a tree—no father, mother, brother, sister. But we know she is rich.

Impossibly short, the scars of rickets obvious in her bowlegs, protruding chin, and nose as big as a donkey's ear, she is unforgettable and definitely ugly—but not in the least repulsive due to her light spirit and biting mockery of herself and others.

She brings gaiety and laughter into our house, telling jokes and droll tales without end, and I always think she's the happiest of souls.

Her house is a ranch for cats and dogs, all born and raised there, all spoiled by her generosity. Each one has a name, an exact feeding schedule, and its own health exercises. She's crazy about them and they're crazy about her. In the abundant mercy of her hospitality, the natural hatred between cats and dogs evaporates and they live together in brotherhood and affection.

"Why has it been so long since we've seen you, Sitt Nagayah?" my mother asks.

She might answer, "Narcissus has been in a bad mood," or "Little Blessing was in labor."

She's always talking about a certain afreet of the jinn who's like a brother to her, and she speaks proudly of their special bond and extolls his exploits. "I felt his breath brush my face just before dawn," she says gravely.

"I found the molasses jug empty, so I told him, 'Welcome and good health to you.'"

This is all honest and serious; the only time she stops joking is to talk about her invisible brother . . .

She also believes dogs and cats talk to her in their own tongues and that she understands them. She switches into dog talk or cat language to prove it and raves on until we're about to die laughing.

So deep is her knowledge of dream interpretation, card reading, and fortune-telling from coffee grounds in overturned cups that she's sometimes accused of practicing sorcery and black magic. Um Abdu even cursed her in public after her daughter Ahsan disappeared, but most people believe she is good . . .

Her dogs keep people from visiting her and servants from staying to help her, so she's alone, but her loneliness is much assuaged by the animals and her brother the afreet.

When she talks about being lonely, my mother says, "People should prepare themselves for Doomsday."

She smiles and answers earnestly: "Dogs will bark around my corpse, cats will meow, and my brother will come to close my eyes. Then Allah may do as He wishes."

27

A guest cries, "Nazzlah! May Allah forgive her!"

My mother says she hasn't yet heard the latest about her, so her visitor goes on. "She chased the poor boy till he fell for her and had to marry her. He took such good care of her that she was the happiest woman in the whole district—but look at her now, the whore, she up and left him just because he got sick!"

This isn't enough for my mother; she encourages the woman to continue. "There he lies, flat in bed, alone, spitting blood and coughing till his lungs burst, wishing he'd die. When I visit him, he says, 'Look, Aunt, what Nazzlah has done.' I comfort him and try to cheer him up, but all the time my heart is breaking . . ."

And I imagine the sick man, the blood, the whorish woman.

Some time later, the woman comes to see my mother again, this time saying, "Will wonders never cease? Hassan died just a few months ago and now the brazen hussy has made his brother Khalil fall for her and marry her."

My mother shouts, "Nazzlah?!"

"Who else? Would anyone else do such a thing? May Allah wreak vengeance upon you, O Nazzlah, daughter of Amuna."

And I conjure up visions of corpse, lover, and whore.

Time passes. I'm in my room studying when I hear my mother greet a guest. "Welcome, Sitt Nazzlah."

Intrigued, I ask myself, "Could this be the whore?"

I sneak down the dark hall and peek into the living room. I see an elegantly dressed woman between forty and fifty with a full body and a beautiful shape. I have to admit she's provocative, worthy of falling in love with. I've recently heard that Khalil, after giving her a son, also died, and that she's moved from their apartment across from the archway to a small place near us. I realize my mother couldn't have been greeting her sincerely, so, after she's gone, I say, "Now there's a wicked woman."

"Allah alone knows what's inside the heart," says my prudent mother.

"You sympathize with her even though you don't welcome her?"

"I've heard a lot, but what I see is a weak woman with a son, no husband, and no money."

Whenever I get a chance, I watch her from my window. I remember the two dead men, Hassan and Khalil, but just don't care, feeling I'm about to start an adventure more dangerous than any I've been through before. But this never gets off the ground . . .

One morning an echoing scream convulses our alley.

Word spreads that a neighbor threw lye in Nazzlah's face and accused her of trying to steal her husband.

Nazzlah loses her charm forever and is forced to take a job in the local bath-house. This makes me sad for a long time, and I repeat my mother's saying: "Allah alone knows what's inside the heart."

28

He visits us often.

I love him because he looks almost exactly like my father. Time after time, with endless persistence, he harangues my father with the question, "Could you stand a situation like mine, Uncle?"

"Mohsen, you must rely on Allah and yourself," my father invariably responds.

"I've inherited a fortune but it's all tied up in the waqf so I can't spend a millieme. That's why I'm so miserable."

"Many heirs are in the same position . . ."

He has to work in the lumberyard for three pounds a month. Restricted by his grim position, he marries Sowsen, not beautiful, not rich, a mere dallala's daughter. Years go by but no children come, so he's filled with regret. Meanwhile his wife begs Allah not to unravel the snarled bequest, telling my mother, "Poverty keeps him from debauchery and stops him from throwing me out . . ."

The waqf is his only topic. "The waqf, Auntie," "Oh, the waqf, Uncle." Again and again, I hear him passionately crying, "Oh Lord, I'm dying to taste choice delicacies, live in a clean place, wear a suit that fits, and have a female—a real female, not a wooden statue disguised as a woman—and, oh Lord, I'm dying for a son, oh!—even a daughter."

As he grows older, his eyes sometimes fill with tears of self-pity that win my sympathy.

Events rush along, changing the rhythm and perception of time, and the knot of the waqf is untied!

My cousin is dancing with joy when I ask how much he'll get.

"Forty thousand pounds," he shouts.

My head spins. I look into his face with wonder. He's almost seventy, white-haired, skinny, near-sighted, and totally toothless. "What are you going to do with all that money?"

Exultant, he cries, "Rejoice in the bounty of the Great and Glorious One! I'll buy Iyusha the midwife's house and a new set of teeth, then get married."

"Get married?"

"Yes, and have children, too, just wait and see."

With great resolve, he rejuvenates himself and remodels his life. He keeps Sowsen but marries Tawheeda, the pickle peddler's daughter, a lovely girl under twenty.

One day he informs me, "If the Merciful permit, the heir apparent is on the way."

He overindulges in food with a gluttony unbecoming to his age and, after six months of marriage, takes to his sickbed.

When I go to him, he says in a faint voice, "I regret nothing, not one thing, thanks be to Allah, Lord of the Two Worlds, Here and Hereafter . . ."

And he orders a beautiful new tomb to be built.

Ali Al-Benan, owner of a coffee-bean shop in our alley, is a friend of mine. When his father died, he took his place though still an adolescent.

I'm keeping him company one day when he asks, "Would you happen to know Onsaya, daughter of Ameena the bakeress?"

With the sharp smell of coffee dominating my senses, I answer, "Well of course. The whole neighborhood knows her."

"What do you think of her?"

"A very attractive girl who helps her mother dutifully."

"Know anything about her character?"

I laugh and answer, "No more than what people say!"

"But I bet a lot of it is true." He adjusts his turban and goes on. "I know her first slip was a tumble with Hamdan the baker's apprentice."

I nod agreeably. In a grave, confessional tone, he says: "And she also got caught with that Hanafi who works in the pickle place under the archway."

"Do you have to talk about it in such a mournful voice?"

"I also have reliable information concerning a connection with a police guard!"

I ask him jokingly, "So? Are you going to write her life story?"

"And even with Hassanayn the water carrier!"

With a boisterous guffaw, I say, "This is conduct deserving solemn contemplation."

"And what's still hidden is probably even worse."

"Who knows? And maybe she's not the only one around, either."

Then he sighs and says: "Maybe not, but she's the only one I love!"

I immediately drop my comic tone. "You want to join the ranks of her lovers?"

He peers at me a long time before he answers. "Absolutely not! I have decided to marry her!"

"I don't believe it."

He becomes doleful and earnestly states, "I've gone through a lot of agony to come to this decision and I won't change my mind no matter what people say."

And Ali Al-Benan carries out his resolve.

Patrick Al-Hamawy enters puberty and wedlock at almost the same moment.

His father, an illiterate contractor, wants to enjoy his last child before he dies, so he picks out a girl when Patrick is a mere student of fourteen. Happy to be a student in more ways than one, Patrick tells tales that ignite the longing and fever the fancies of his peers.

He does well enough in school to go on with higher studies. Then he gets sent to England for two years. When he comes back, he can't fit into his old life.

The worst problem is his wife. They disagree about everything, and her ignorance and superstition drive him first to distraction, then to alienation and despair. "Life can't go on like this," he tells people.

After a long struggle, he finally decides to divorce her.

Every tongue in the alley wags insults and curses, but he calmly braves the hostile tide and then throws in an even greater challenge by bringing home a new wife, a foreigner. He claims she's French, but the alley swears she's just a Lebanese Greek!

People look at her shiny unveiled face with hate and disgust, and the devout ones pray for the soul of Patrick's father, Hamawy the muallim, notable and good.

Troublesome questions about the new wife's behavior rise and circulate. Doesn't she mix with men a bit too freely? Don't you think she drinks a bit too much? Can her version of Islam possibly be considered correct? Are her children getting a proper Islamic upbringing?

Patrick Al-Hamawy suffers through all this, faces it with every ounce of strength and disdain he can muster.

But problems in his own house crush him without mercy. His wife gets fed up with her neighbors and starts attacking their traditions with scorn and sarcasm. And the minute Patrick gives in to one of her demands, she asks for something else. He ends up admitting he's eardeep in misery.

People advise him to divorce her and leave everything to Allah.

"I can't accept defeat," he answers stubbornly, and when she offers to divorce him, he refuses out of pride.

Then one day she just takes off, leaving Patrick, the neighborhood, and the country.

For years Patrick never gives a thought to marriage. It exasperates him when relatives suggest he get his first wife back. "That's ridiculous!"

"Well, then, how about the second one?"

"Utter madness!" Then from a grave meditation, he adds, "Marriage is a must, the earlier the better. It wasn't all for naught since now at least I know what I want."

31

The tale of Sayeeda Kareem is one of the most touching love stories in the quarter.

A chaste and honest love secretly springs up between her and Idrees Al-Qadi, a neighbor's son. In spite of their bashful discretion, looks of love betray them and incite an argument between Sheikh Kareem, learned teacher of Arabic, and Am Hassanayn, vendor of sweets.

"Tell your son to mind his manners."

"My son is *never* improper."

One word leads to another and then another. When words are about to become actions, peacemakers step in. But now spies are put on guard, all eyes are peeled, and the subjugated lovers suffer in silence.

When Idrees completes high school, he convinces his father to ask the Sheikh for Sayeeda's hand. The reluctant father goes and makes the request.

Dryly, the sheikh says, "Your son is just another student in no position to marry, and my daughter can't wait around."

But to his loyal adherents, the sheikh says, "How can he even dream of being related to me, that petty peddler?"

Then the son of a good family, decent and suitable, asks for Sayeeda's hand.

But Sayeeda rejects him! Refusal is rare, no easy business. Her revolt baffles the surprised sheikh and his neighbors. The whole family rocks with rage, riot, and rebuke, but Sayeeda sticks to her refusal, even telling her father she's merely exercising her religious right!

In their usual wicked way, alley tongues blab rumors and conjectures, creating silly fables that eventually reach the sheikh's ears. Heavy sorrow rides him, old age reaches out to him, and, one day in the middle of a lesson, death kidnaps him.

Sayeeda suffers. Her family and the community at large blame her for her father's death. She is cursed, persecuted, considered evil-omened, and avoided like the plague.

Years slip by with no one proposing to her.

When Idrees finishes college, he begs his sweetheart's uncle for

Sayeeda's hand but meets a glowering rejection. Even her mother won't approve.

Years pass, light and few to those who count and compute, long and heavy to those who ache. Sayeeda is a virtual prisoner, Idrees a government official whose bachelorhood raises bureaucratic eyebrows. Their close friends never doubt that their love will last, defying every obstacle.

Idrees is sent to work in other Arab countries. Nobody hears anything about him for years. Sayeeda's spring glow fades and she comes to look like misery incarnate.

In his mid-fifties, Idrees returns to Egypt, a man with a forgotten past. The few who do remember no longer find it of any interest. But our alley does sniff out something unusual: Idrees is still a bachelor, he's never been married, never known what it means to be a father.

And he goes to Sayeeda's mother and asks for her hand!

Everyone is amazed since Sayeeda, they point out, is not exactly a groom-pleaser anymore.

And the wedding takes place, crowning two lives melted away by fidelity, perseverance, and pain.

32

Senan Shalaby works in the flour mill next to the old fountain. He happens to glance through the window of a nearby house and catch a glimpse of a face so fascinating that it rules his fate. His bewitched heart masters his will with a power he never dreamed possible. "You've gone nuts, Senan, and that's all there is to it," he mutters to himself.

As far as he can tell, the lovely face never leaves the house. A woman familiar in the alley, Um Saad, goes out to bargain and market for the household. No one knows what kind of relationship Um Saad and the beauty have because they neither visit nor receive, but there's plenty of speculation around. Um Saad might be the beauty's mother or some other relative. Maybe she's just her servant. Oh, and who's this Saad anyway, Um Saad's son? Where's he? Then the rumors get ugly.

Senan Shalaby says, "I want her, I'm crazy about her, and by good or evil I mean to have her—even if I have to pay with my priceless life."

So when Um Saad comes to shop at the mill, he scrapes an acquaintance with her. She ignores his little hints about this fantastic desire of his while at the same time encouraging him to give her small, cheap presents like leban, hanteet, and sugar. At last she tells him, "The jewel is expensive and you're a man of limited means."

Even as poverty shrinks his heart, madness expands it. "God will help us."

He now realizes the beauty is a professional lover but doesn't care. Insane passion clutches his will so tightly he has no choice, no time for scruples.

"This deal isn't easy," Um Saad says. "There are guards you don't see. All I can do is show you the way." She spreads her palm suggestively and Senan puts a silver five-piaster coin in it. She scorns the offering, won't take less than ten, a tithe of his monthly salary. "You know the Muallim Halambuhah, don't you? Tell him I sent you. He takes care of her and commands her. He brought her out of the unknown and into our alley."

Senan is peeved. "I thought you were going to help me sidestep the go-between."

"All I can do is show you the way."

Senan goes to the tiny shop where Halambuhah sells tobacco and opium. He's old, blear-eyed, shriveled of soul, just as he has been for as long as Senan can remember. The moment their greetings are over, Senan whispers, "Um Saad sent me."

With an angry scowl, Halambuhah snarls, "One Egyptian pound!"

"It's a huge price, oh Muallim," says Senan in dismay.

Halambuhah looks off in another direction and says, "Save your money and go away."

But nothing can douse the fire inside Senan Shalaby. He bows to the inevitable, sells a ring inherited from his father for one pound, and pays Halambuhah. The old man inspects the money, stuffs it into his pocket, and says: "Now the only one left is Hareedy Hamilowi. Know him?"

Senan's heart sinks. "What's he got to do with it?"

"He's her fiancé. Won't take less than two pounds."

"But that's a fortune," groans Senan, "and this is a chain without end . . ."

"Hareedy is the last link."

"But how will I get my hands on two pounds?"

"So take your money and go!" Furious, he throws the pound back at Senan, who trudges away squashed and glum.

His legs direct him to the booza. Senan gets so soused he ends up telling himself, "I'll get what I want even if I have to jump over clouds . . ."

And he hurries drunkenly off to Um Elish, an egg peddler who lives in a wooden shack on Um Ali's roof. She's annoyed to see him.

"Hey, I don't do business in my room . . ."

All of a sudden, he throws himself on her with all his might, stifles her, smothers her, leaves her a corpse . . .

* * * * *

He knows very well he ought to run away before someone discovers the murder, for many people must have seen him stagger up to the house of Um Ali the midwife. He knows quite well but thinks of nothing but love.

He goes straight to Muallim Halambuhah and hands over the pound, then on to Hareedy Hamilowi with two pounds. Hareedy escorts him to the house of Um Saad.

* * * * *

And those who tell this story say Senan entering the room of his beloved was a man ascending to Paradise. Joyous with drink, he cast his body at her feet in frenzy. He knew that he wept with passion, that and no more. This moment of high exultation so flooded him with bright truth and honesty that he said, "I have done murder . . ."

The beloved didn't understand him at all and he never consummated the act. But not till first light dawned did he become aware of the passage of time.

Then from the street below rose up a noise. Feet stomped heavily on the stairs and Senan, as if receiving a secret signal, submitted willingly to the Fates . . .

33

Our alley goes through a period that might be called the Age of Zenab.

Her father peddles fruit, her mother eggs. Zenab is the last grape in a cluster of males. She's beautiful, fabulously so, and in this lies her story.

When she was a baby, her family passed her from hand to hand like a toy, and she gleamed with hints of great beauty even in childhood. By early youth she was a paragon of bright splendor.

Her father Zedan orders his wife to keep her secluded in the house at all times. Her mother agrees this isn't a bad idea—but grudgingly, since she wishes Zenab could go out and earn her own way, if only that were possible.

So many suitors fawn and drool like dogs over her that the family is embarrassed. Her mother says, "Well, it's only simple justice for her beauty to form her future."

So, imagining a great match, the mother turns down her sister's son, a mere horse-cart driver. This breaks family ties and starts a feud that is minutely observed by the whole alley, the curious, the reproachful, and the malign.

Then Hassan and Khaleel, apprentices to the butcher and the tarboosh maker, propose to her at almost the same time. They get into a nasty fistfight and do each other permanent injury.

Right after this, Farag Idduri the schoolteacher asks for her hand. Since he's respectable, a gentleman and an official, a dream of dreams given Zenab's background, her mother announces, "This is the man we favor for our daughter."

But one day Ali the waterpot peddler blocks the teacher's path and whispers, "If you like living, stay away from Zenab."

For protection, the teacher calls in a rugged cousin of his who's used to threats and brawls. He proceeds to give the waterpot peddler a good pounding. But Ali holds a silent grudge. One day he ambushes Farag Effendi and pokes his eye out!

For the sake of peace, all decent folk in the neighborhood give up their proposals. No one is left in the ring but gangsters and tough guys.

The infuriated mother screams, "What rotten luck!"

Thugs and bullies drub each other. Every day someone else gets bashed and the menace mounts. Out of fear of reprisal, the Zedan family tries to maintain strict neutrality. Despite these trials and tribulations, some people still jinx them by saying they're very lucky! "Lucky?" says Zedan to his friends. "We're being wiped out by a curse called beauty!"

The battle rages on, more men get hurt, and Zenab and her family come to embody a curse that causes hatred, envy, resentment, and the craving for revenge.

Zedan never draws a breath in peace, afraid one of these evil ruffians will act treacherously with Zenab herself and ruin her forever . . .

One morning we can't find the slightest trace of the Zedans. Dejection and sadness descend. I suffer from a frustration no one notices. "Is it impossible," I ask myself sadly, "for beauty to thrive in our alley?"

34

One of the heroines of neighborhood love stories is Henaya, daughter of Alwana the dallala.

I often wonder what she sees in Hamam, an ugly gallabiya maker's apprentice with a bad reputation and a foul temper. He goes naked under his gallabiya and walks around barefoot while Henaya, on the other hand, is an educated young lady; she stayed in mosque school for three years to learn to make out words, add figures, and recite all the short suras by heart. Her mother is so well-off she can afford to fry food; the aroma spreads from their kitchen at lunchtime.

When Hamid the sabot salesman proposes, Henaya refuses. Her mother tells my mother about this tragedy through feverish tears. "Just imagine! Hamid, the perfect match, a man of wealth."

"How can it be? She's a sensible girl who's studied God's word."

"They say someone cast a spell on her. To get rid of it, I went to Sheikh Labeeb, visited the usual shrines, and made vows."

But Henaya remains adamant about her refusal. Her mother smacks her face and screams, "You prefer a criminal? Never! You must be fated for misery."

When Hamid finally gives up and goes away, Hamam starts thinking that marriage is serious; it's expensive and will mean being responsible in dress and behavior. Just then he's accused of mugging someone, caught, and stuck in jail for two years.

Alwana the dallala is overjoyed with this solution, a blessing from heaven, and tells Henaya: "See? Praise be to Allah! No proof is greater than His proof."

But Henaya still won't marry Hamid. She's so unhappy that even people who were angry at her begin to feel sorry for her. They say happiness isn't possible for her because jerking Hamam out of her heart will leave a scar. The two years pass and Hamam comes home. Henaya is filled with life again and her mother's insane rage grows wilder. Hamam can't get his old job back or find a new one. Then, suddenly, he's walking around with a tray of headmeat for sale. Everybody wonders where he got the scratch to go into business, but no one finds out till later that Henaya gave him one of her gold bracelets.

Alwana throws a horrendous fit and calls on all her neighbors and relatives to help her against her daughter, but Henaya marries Hamam in the police station under official protection.

I can swear it's a successful marriage. Henaya helps Hamam in his work, directing it with a wisdom far beyond his scatterbrained methods.

Eventually he—or, to be precise, she—is able to open a shop. And as for the old memories, no one finds it necessary to bring them up anymore.

35

When a day for cemetery visits comes around, we sometimes go to an enclosure not far from our own. In the room set aside for holiday feasts, I see a man who must be living there since I notice a bed, sofa, and table. I ask my mother who he is and she answers, "That's Radwan Effendi, your father's cousin."

"Why is he staying here?"

She ignores my question. A year later the room is empty and I find out he has moved from the room to the tomb itself. Later still, on some occasion I can't recall, I hear his story.

Radwan Effendi and his wife had a son and a daughter. The mother adored the boy, the father the girl. When they were adolescents, the boy, in the name of manhood and self-respect, used his strength to bully his sister and make her life unbearable. His father got so mad at him their relationship fell apart—or, as my mother put it, "The devil lived between them."

The dispute became a dirty struggle. The father inflicted discipline without mercy and the son returned insolence without restraint until nothing but blind hate bound them, each wishing for the other's annihilation and ruin.

Soon after finishing high school, the boy became consumptive and, six months later, died. It was a harsh death, harboring so much cunning, betrayal, and irony that the mother's hope in life vanished and she collapsed. An earthquake of regret and fear rocked the father, who told my father, "It's like having your pocket picked. I can't face his mother for the shame of it."

And a year after the son's death, the daughter came down with the same illness.

Radwan Effendi came running to us one night from the other side of the quarter, barefoot, hair a mess, eyes bloodshot. The family knew, as they rose to question him, what he was going to say. Panting, the light of life smothered in his eyes, the man told them, "It's all over."

He gave up business and left his home for the graveyard to be near the tombs of his children. His life insisted on dragging itself out until his appointed hour.

The mother still visits us. I watch her and, though she is old and I am young, become close to her.

She seems to have forgotten the past and loves to while away the time by reading the future in cards. I can see us now: she sits before a spread of cards and I hunch eagerly in front of her. She's showing me a face-card and saying, "I perceive on your road a person not of your blood."

She smiles so much that I tell my mother, "Auntie Waleeda is cheerful and loves to laugh."

My mother murmurs, "Our Lord be with her and all wounded souls."

36

One sleepless night I watch this scene from my window.

A man's figure staggers around and smashes into walls. He stumbles, falls, and gets up again with a great effort. Then a most eloquent song gushes from his mouth:

> I was a woman hitherto,
> A dimwit dunce to dither to.

Then like a bull agallop to gore, he charges to do battle with an invisible foe, loses his balance, and sprawls on the ground like a corpse.

Some kind people notice him, and one of them, apparently a baker, picks him up and spreads him out on a huge bread board. The others help him lift the board and carry it.

After only a few steps, they meet another drunk, staggering, stumbling, standing, falling. From his perch on the bread board, the first drunk guffaws and yells: "Yuck, what a bum you are! You drink till you can't stand up and make yourself a local laughingstock. Eeeychch!"

Later, under very serious circumstances, this scene comes back to me heavy with implications that never occurred to me at the time.

37

Am Yansoon Issuramati is an old man with a spotless reputation. After a short illness, his son Ramadan dies. Naturally, the old man is struck down by grief, but, with his face still wet with tears, he does something so strange it makes him the talk of the whole quarter. All anyone knows is that he signs an engagement contract with Daleela, his dead son's fiancée, and then goes and marries her before even one month has passed.

Has he gone mad?

And even if he has, why can't he wait a year or so?

And how can Daleela accept a man forty years her senior?

But there's no doubt about it, it's happened. Daleela moves into Am Yansoon's house and lives with him and the rest of his family, first wife included.

Tongues writhe and whisper: there must have been something between the girl and the dead Ramadan only a quick wedding could conceal; they must have trusted a future that never arrived; death turned everything upside-down and put Daleela in a helpless, hopeless fix.

Daleela's mother knew her secret, it seems, and told Ramadan's mother, who, in turn, laid it on her mourning husband's back—a new catastrophe, a catastrophe in every sense of the word. He could hardly ignore it; the girl was in a jam, and his son, to whose memory mercy must be shown, was the guilty cause of it. So he thought and thought and finally decided to make the most unusual marriage in alley history.

Daleela delivers her son in his house.

A few people bless what he has done and pray all goes well with them.

Others, in ignorance and innocence, accuse him of being a mad old fool.

And those fond of sarcasm point at him and whisper, "There goes the father of his own grandson."

38

I'm playing in the alley when, from the Iddeeb house, a trilling-cry rings out. Several people say, "God willing, we're about to get some good news."

Sure enough, someone comes to announce that a marriage contract between Naain Issaqaf and Sheikhun Iddehl has been agreed upon.

The word reaches Fathaya Qaysoon as she's doing her wash in a big tub in front of her building. She leaps up as if stung, unties her gallabiya, knots her headscarf and madly stuffs a few stray hairs into it, then grabs her long black malaya from a rock and throws it over herself, flapping its sides like the wings of a bird of prey. She shakes fists full of menace, arches her head in a stance of attack, and finally tears away, sure of where she's headed, screaming: "By the prophet! And by the prophet of prophets! I'll muddy his life! I'll rip his face into such a horror even his own mother won't know him!"

And away she goes, leaving a wake of bloody expectations, feverish wishes to know what will happen, and feelings that veer between pity and malice.

39

Sabri Gawani's name never fails to rouse a storm of questions.

He comes from a background of drudgery and works in a notions shop. Then he gets chosen to go around to similar shops in nearby districts. Virtually overnight, he loses his habitual pallor, improves his health, and puts on the prosperous dress of success. We often see him hauling packages of meat and fruit into his new house. He spends his afternoons in the coffeehouse smoking a hookah and drinking ginger tea, and he sometimes stays up late at one of Mowaweely's hashish parties.

Then he marries a girl of good family and wears a suit instead of a gallabiya. His face glows with contentment, confidence, and security. And on the night of his friend Al-Halag's wedding, he gets plastered, he dances, he sings—in short, does everything a happy man *should* do.

After the wedding procession, he leaves the party to go back home. But he never gets there.

He vanishes without a trace, without so much as a word.

40

Behind a barred window he sits and stares at nothing, his eyes meaningless stones. Once in a while his small, bald head manages to mumble, "O darling, where are you?"

Curious, we peer at him from a distance, careful not to get him excited. We've been warned about that.

"Look at his eyes!" we whisper.

"What's he mean by that?"

"He's crazy."

Every time he saw a veiled woman, he would silently dog her footsteps and, when he got a chance, jump out in front of her and block her way. People say he fell in love with a beautiful girl in a dream. Again and again she came to him in the dream, so he began to wander the streets to find her.

But then he got impatient and started tearing women's veils off, which of course made people angry, and they would subdue him.

His relatives decided he must be bewitched and took him to the appropriate shrines and to Sheikh Labeeb, but the sheikh saw no hope for him.

People came to his father. "There are hospitals for those like your son. It's fate. Give up on him."

Instead, his father locked him in his room and barred the windows.

So he spends his days staring through the bars at nothing; he grows old, still occasionally mumbling, "O darling, where are you?"

41

The most gargantuan human frame I've ever seen belongs to Ibrahim the Ape. I can't imagine a taller or broader man existing any time, any place. A minaret, he picks his way around by poking with a dreadful great staff, his feet shuffling along like immense turtles beneath him. Our alley believes his blindness is really a sign of God's mercy.

When he turned his hand to begging, all other beggars quit the vicinity because none of them dared repeat the formula, "For the love of God, good people, for Allah," when he was around.

Propped up against his staff, he sits cross-legged just outside the vaulted archway, silent for hours at a stretch. Then he'll suddenly thunder, "Generous patrons!" That and no more. His meals arrive on a fixed schedule, milliemes pile up in his pocket, and he exchanges pleasantries with passers-by.

The contrast between his mighty strength and his puny profession does make people chuckle a bit, though not—since he's native to our alley and never throws his weight around—with resentment or malice.

I happen to be there the day of his great battle.

It's grave-visiting season again, and Zalooma, another blind beggar, comes into our alley through the archway from the cemetery. He's had a good day, but tiring as well, so, weary with the weight of dates and pastry, he decides to rest a while on a spot near the Ape. There they sit, two blind beggars, sentinels on each side of the arch. The Ape's sharp

ears pick up the soft smack and munch of Zalooma's lips, his nose drinks in seductive smells from Zalooma's huge package of food, and he turns his head toward the source with intent curiosity and anticipation.

But Zalooma chooses that very moment to shout out one of his favorite formulas: "O Hussein, beloved of the Prophet, master of martyrs, succor!"

Ibrahim the Ape, gruff and frowning, asks, "Who's there?"

"Nobody but one asking for a bit of generosity," Zalooma answers in all innocence.

"Who brought you here, you son of a bitch?"

"So Allah's earth is yours?" Zalooma retorts.

"Can't you see me?"

"I see only the light of the heart."

Ibrahim the Ape mutters, "Wonderful," gets up, spreads his hands, and goes toward Zalooma as straight as if he were able to see him. He grabs Zalooma's arms and, though I can't see what he does to him, I do see the poor man thrashing around, twisting and screaming for help.

A crowd gathers and pulls them apart, no easy task. Some in the crowd make angry remarks.

"Unfair."

"Tyrannical."

"Monster."

"Where's your fear of God?"

Ibrahim the Ape yells, "Damn all of you!"

Someone loses his temper and throws a broken basket at him.

At that, the Ape rebels. His revolt is more impressive than most mass demonstrations, an exploding ball. He gets madder and madder, spews the ugliest insults he can think of, then extends his staff and spins around, clobbering everything and everybody inside an ever-growing circle of terror. The crowd scatters. Running in low crouches, men crash into each other, fall, scream, and shout for help. Soon the Ape is a blind destructive force that engulfs the whole alley. People hurry to shut up shops and dive down small lanes out of sight. Chairs and wares are shattered, baskets toppled right and left.

The police burst into the alley. Astonished to learn the troublemaker is merely a blind beggar, the chief officer blithely orders his arrest.

The battle is rejoined, now between Ape and police, who, as ordered, use no weapons. They therefore go sailing through the air like so many toys. The Ape is invincible.

Young boys gather at the fringes of the fray to egg the Ape on with inspiring cheers. I've never seen a government force reduced to such a mess before. Out of the white uniform with red ribbon comes the shout of the chief, "Hey, Ape! Give up right now or you'll be shot!"

Drunk with victory, the Ape doesn't even slow down. Mercifully, the officer doesn't order his men to open fire or even use truncheons but instead calls out the fire department.

Water gushes out of the hose, an inescapable cascade. The Ape is confused. He stumbles, spins around in staggers, and finally—defeated, bitter, and still hurling filthy insults—falls flat on the ground, helpless. The cops pounce on him with handcuffs.

For quite a while the Ape steers clear of our neighborhood, but one day he comes back with all his mass and height on full, proud display. Cordial greetings and warm welcomes hail his return. He takes up his old life, parking his enormous frame at the archway like a myth.

42

Bergowi is dedicated to his work in the falafel shop.

Kefrowi happens by one day and asks for a drink of water. A funny whim grabs Bergowi, and he points to the donkey trough. "There you go. Help yourself."

When some customers snicker, Kefrowi gets mad. "You're an uncouth bastard!" he shouts.

This makes Bergowi angry too. "So to hell with you and all your ancestors!"

They fire insults at each other, and a group of watchers of all ages gathers. The imam of the mosque tries to calm things down, but when no one pays attention to him, he stalks away in a huff.

The battle heats up. Kefrowi grabs a brick and heaves it at the shop. When it breaks the big gas lamp hanging from the ceiling, Bergowi loses all control of himself, grabs the falafel pan, and beats Kefrowi over the head with it till he's dead.

The Bergowi and Kefrowi clans swarm to the scene and start a bloody battle. Bricks, clubs, and knives are put to work. Several men get killed and the rest end up in jail.

For a long time I never see anything but women dressed in black in the houses of both Bergowi and Kefrowi. This makes me feel sorry, of course, and I say what should be said in such situations.

But a number of people in our neighborhood honor the memory of this ruinous riot and tell tales of the bloody fight with a pride utterly disdainful of jails and gallows.

Hawash Adad is one of the big spenders in our part of town.

He decides to throw a huge holiday bash at his house and sends invitations to his numerous cronies, to local big shots, and to singers and dancers both classy and cheap. The strings begin to vibrate and the music spreads an uproar through the air, arousing an itch in the uninvited and choler among the pious.

Racket and song go on till dawn when all at last totter off to sleep.

In the morning, the alley is bubbling over with festival joy when weird noises and terrified screams burst from Hawash Adad's house as if it's been hit by lightning.

People rush toward the house all agape, and then comes the story—a thing never heard of before.

Those who tell the tale say that host and guests woke to find themselves scattered at random in a world of such utter havoc it beggars both imagination and description. They remember falling asleep full of joy, feeling perfect, but they open their eyes to the results of an earthquake. Expensive furniture lies in splinters; sofas, sideboards, chairs, and tables are decimated, their pieces in small heaps all over the place; cushions, armrests, curtains, and upholstery are ripped to shreds, and their stuffing floats around in big flakes; jugs, bottles, glasses, plates, braziers, and waterpipes are smashed, bits of them strewn everywhere. Not a lantern, knickknack, carpet, rug, or piece of loose clothing has escaped the ravage. What happened? Why? How?

The police come, hunt for clues, and take depositions without explaining a thing. Some people suggest that a drunken quarrel became a riotous free-for-all, destroying everything, but that the big shots persuaded the police to hush it up; still, nobody got hurt—so how could that be?

Others say Hawash's enemies drugged the revelers and then savagely wrecked everything in sight; still, wouldn't it be more logical to take revenge on the people themselves? Almost no one buys that version.

One rumor afloat says the wrath of God caused it, that Hawash, the profligate and frivolous, deserved what he got. Supposedly, host and guests, befuddled and semi-conscious, demolished the place themselves and then fell into a dead sleep.

This version finds open ears and so does a similar one: the jinn did it because of a vow Hawash made and never fulfilled.

Days and years go by and no one in the neighborhood ever men-

tions the incident without exclaiming, "God have mercy!" or "Allah is the source of all strength!" and praying for protection from the devil.

44

This story is from old times; I didn't see it myself.

A small mosque, with a man named Sheikh Aml Al-Mahdi as imam, had just been built. One night when the sheikh went up into the minaret to call for dawn prayers, a voice from a house across the way caught his ear. He turned to see a woman open a window and a man crush his hand over her mouth to stifle her cry for help. Then he jerked her back inside where, under the full glare of a gaslight, he flung himself upon her and battered her with something in his hand till she fell down dead.

The sheikh knew them both. The woman was Sitt Sikeena, widow of the owner of a falafel shop, and the man was Mohamed Al-Zumr, a muallim, a potentate, a respected man, who owned the lumberyard.

Sheikh Aml Al-Mahdi was nailed to the spot, shrouded in darkness, limbs atremble, till the muallim shut the window. He mumbled over and over, "He's killed her, surely he's killed her."

His voice failed him and he couldn't make the prayer call.

A murder! What was the muallim doing in the lady's house at such an hour? Ah, there's more than one crime here—Oh God of heaven and earth, have mercy on us!

He struggled shakily down the spiral staircase and sat on the floor with his back against the pulpit. The first worshippers to arrive were shocked by the way he looked.

"Why didn't we hear your voice this morning, Sheikh Aml?" some of them asked.

Gasping, he answered, "I'm sick—Allah knows best."

And he was sick, for it was none other than Muallim Mohamed Al-Zumr who paid for the mosque to be built, who chose Sheikh Aml to be imam, who paid his salary. The sheikh pondered this and said to himself, "Oh, what a hard test from Allah the All-Knowing."

And he sat in his house three days without opening his mouth.

Word of the crime flew through the alley. Everyone soon knew Sitt Sikeena was found in her bedroom, in her nightgown, murdered. At the inquest, Sheikh Aml, among others, was called to the stand.

"You didn't hear a scream or anything at all unusual when you went up to make the prayer call?" asked the examining magistrate.

"I was too sick to do it that night."

"You live right next door to the murdered woman. Don't you know anything about her relations with anyone?"

"All I know is that she was a respectable lady."

He left the inquest telling himself he was forever damned and began to sob violently from sorrow and weakness.

The detectives discovered that a few pieces of jewelry were missing and so became suspicious of an assistant in the laundry who sometimes went to the lady's house. They searched his place, found the baubles, and accused him of murder.

This looked eminently logical to everyone but Sheikh Aml, who followed the investigation with maniacal intensity. He burned right down to the marrow of his bones, mangling his nerves. Though he was pious and devout, his piety and fear of God were one thing, his courage another.

Worry and grief got the best of him and broke him down; feebleness invaded every fiber of his being.

Then one day in front of the ancient fountain, he ran into Muallim Mohamed Al-Zumr. He shook hands with him as usual but then began to tremble as if he had touched a snake, staring at the muallim with a look so dark and deep that he asked, "What's wrong with you, Sheikh Aml?"

The sheikh found himself saying, "Allah was watching you!"

The muallim was amazed. "What do you mean? Are you sick?"

Then the sheikh shouted at him, "Confess your crime, you murderer!" and rushed into the mosque, locking the door behind him with bolt and key.

For two whole days he stayed in his prison without responding to his family or anyone else.

At sunset on the third day, he surprised everyone by appearing at the minaret's high window. But what an appearance! People looked up at him with faces full of dismay and repeated, over and over, "There is no power or strength but in God."

"The good man is utterly naked."

"Sheikh Aml, God is One! Find strength in that!"

But he just went on staggering around that high little room, swaying and chanting in a voice full of rattles:

Why did you fall into a love so deep
If its promises you couldn't keep?

There's a worker in our saddlery named Ashur Iddenf, about forty, a married father of ten. His most obvious traits are immense strength, tough looks, and wretched poverty. From dawn till midnight, always hungry and tired, he toils away, strangling in anguish whenever rich folks enter the cafe or a whiff of roast meat surprises his nose. He envies the donkey at the saddlery mill every bit as much as the perfumer or lumberyard owner.

One day he remarks to our imam, "Allah creates wealth but neglects my children."

The enraged imam shouts back: "Our prophet Mohamed, God bless and grant him salvation, spent several nights with a big stone bound tight against his stomach to still the pangs of hunger, so get out of here, God damn you!"

*   *   *   *   *

Around midnight Ashur Iddenf is on his way home from work, plowing through darkness, when he hears a soft voice whispering, "Hey, Am Ashur!"

He stops and turns to face a closed ground-floor window in Sitt Fadeela's house; she's a lucky widow who's about to inherit the Shananeery family waqf. "Who's that?" he asks.

"I want you to do something for me. Come in," says the voice.

It's so dark the stuffed crocodile over the door is only a dim outline. He goes under it and finds the sitting room by following a ray of light that glimmers from a peephole in its door. Sitt Fadeela, legs crossed, relaxes on a Turkish sofa. He stands there in front of her, exuding the crude pungence of his sweat. To him, she's a lush cow, provocative and appetizing—but also a lady, modest and respectable, so his insides churn with clashing emotions. The woman says, "I need some cake and oil."

She says it artlessly, with a fake stupidity that betrays an innocent guile. But her scarlet face confesses for her, and Ashur sees in the droop of her eyelids the miracle of consent and submission. But it isn't the submission that comes to him first, not at all, for she's still quite untouchable, absolutely in control of herself, a prudent schemer. So by the time he leaves, he understands she wants him legally!

*   *   *   *   *

He can't believe it and for a long time thinks he must have tripped into a dream, but he does marry the rich widow. Our alley starts talking about him as the great exception to the rule, a rarity, a great example. As the marriage contract stipulates, he quits his saddlery job and permits, without protest, a clause that allows her to divorce him. Then, in a new suit, new skin, and the halo of wealth, he presents himself before us. As Sitt Fadeela wished, he keeps his first wife. Since she and her children receive a generous monthly allowance, they bless the marriage from the bottom of their hearts. And so Ashur Iddenf lives the world he'd always dreamed of, happy and replete.

*   *   *   *   *

Sitt Fadeela turns out to be not just beautiful but perfect as well. She loves him, takes excellent care of him, and makes him a new man. She's gracious, well-bred, and faithful but won't give up even the tiniest bit of his life.

Right from the first Ashur feels she wants total possession of his surface and core, both self and shadow, every thought and dream. In garden or guest room, outside or in, no matter: he lives between her two hands. Even when he spends an hour in the coffeehouse, he spots her shadow against the windowpane, peering in on him. But in spite of this he goes on basking in love, comfort, and satisfaction.

*   *   *   *   *

Once Ashur grows used to good things and clothes the miracle of plenty in habit, boredom seeps into his soul. He develops a craving to be alone and wanders aimlessly, stopping, perhaps, to joke with a friend or take part in some innocent silliness, but he still feels watched, subjugated, stalked. True, he lacks nothing, but he's a prisoner just the same. Silk chains to replace his old iron ones draw tighter on his throat and boredom floods him. Time he finds long, time he finds heavy, time he finds a foe.

One days he says to her, "Open me a shop."

"What for? You have everything you could possibly want."

"Every man works, even beggars," he complains.

He believes she's afraid that if he starts working he'll become financially independent and be able to do without her; all he really wants is a chance to get out from under her fixed stare.

*   *   *   *   *

Ashur Iddenf goes back to griping and complaining, just as in the old days. His tongue rattles out proverbs of injustice, wrong, and the consequences to those who commit them.

When his anger boils over and he decides to do as he pleases, winds of discord blow the calm of the happy house away. At last his exasperation gets the better of him, and he slaps her on the right cheek. She boots him out of heaven and, defiant, he leaves.

* * * * *

After his expulsion, he faces many problems and has a hard time making a living at all. He's forced to go into some dubious business and one day gets beaten up at the police station.

Then the lady feels sorry for him and proposes peaceful reconciliation on the old terms. But, more than once, he adamantly refuses her to go his own tiresome, troublestrewn way.

And Ashur is thus justly hailed as a rarity of an extraordinary new type in our alley.

46

I was taking care of Saad Al-Gebaly during his last illness when a busker's song arose from the street. "You brought it on yourself with your own hand, my heart."

Saad drew breath, smiled, and murmured, "Yes, it's true. I swear it, with your own hand, my heart."

We looked at each other and thought of his life, rich in adventure, pleasure, and pain.

* * * * *

He clerked at the local money lender's but dreamed big dreams. So he sold a piece of land he happened to own, quit his job, and set himself up in perfumery. He did quite well and became one of the most prosperous people around.

But he never developed any merchant thrift. He'd invite friends to his house every night, spread food and drink before them, and play the oud for their amusement. Someone with a nice voice would sing, and the party would last till midnight.

Then he guessed wrong on an investment and, without enough

saved up to cover the deficit, declared himself bankrupt, placing himself—wife, kids, brother—at God's door.

He went through times rocky and rough enough to harm his health
and hurt his pride, but he never lost the look of a strong and stable man.
He went back to work at the money lender's, gave private lessons in
math, and lived an ascetic life.

His faith is strong and deep.

True, he still drinks quite a bit and isn't exactly a paragon of piety
and prayer, but he's no less a true believer for that. To escape what is
written is impossible. Nothing will happen to him that hasn't been
ordained by God.

And nothing can keep him away from work until he falls so ill he
can't get out of bed.

The condition of his family fills me with sorrow. I gesture toward
some of his children at play in the room and say, "May Allah make you
healthy for their sake."

"My health is forever ruined," he says with resignation. "And as for
the kids," he struggles to go on, "I'm not worried about them, and they
don't grieve."

He points his finger upward and says, "Fear is blasphemy. God
protect us from fear. Do you really suppose," he scoffs, "that my life
has fed them so my death can starve them?"

Such strong faith utterly fascinates me.

But even in this far extremity of trouble, Saad Al-Gebaly doesn't
forget to joke. So when the busker belts out his line, Saad smiles and
murmurs, "Yes, by God, with your own hand, my heart."

47

And then there's Shalaby Ilaly, whose story ought to be a poetic
elegy. Nothing else can do it justice.

He's a man both gentle and lovable, but he harps on the same theme
to the point of eccentricity: his admiration for his father. Now pride in
one's father is a long way from unusual in our part of town, but anyone
who overindulges in anything will sooner or later attract some jibes. His
father was a mere clerk in a notions shop, but he was tall and broad—
and in our alley men are judged by width and length.

One day Shalaby sighs and says to me, "I guess I still see my father
through a child's eyes—or even through my mother's eyes!"

"Well, that happens to lots of us."

"Yes, but a boy usually grows up and follows his father's profession, which gives him a chance to see him as he really is. But I went to grade school and high school instead, so my father just stuck there in my imagination, a myth . . ."

"What kind of myth?"

"A myth of glory and wealth!" He stops for a moment but goes on. "But when he died a veil was ripped apart and I found a strange world."

"Strange world?"

"He didn't leave us a single millieme. That was a shocker. I figured he must have been over-generous to the poor . . ."

He goes on telling me—or confessing to me—that after he'd landed a government job, he decided it'd be nice to have the grain dealer's daughter to wife. Wishing to put his best foot forward, he proudly proclaimed to the dealer that he was the son of Alaly.

"His refusal absolutely flooded me! I dug around for some reason for it and finally found the answer in my father's memoirs."

"Really?"

"You can't imagine how I felt."

Scrabbling around the dead man's grave, he had indeed found some sour secrets, but the most important is that as a young man his father had been accused of theft, convicted, and jailed for a year. The notions shop owner had hired him only because they'd been close friends for a long time.

Shalaby Alaly broods over his worries alone, not even telling his mother, who knows nothing about all this, and shows me his buried skeletons not to share his troubles with someone but merely because he imagines his father's tale is something every droll tongue is already clucking over.

The naked facts ram a brutal contradiction through the center of his life. On one hand he leads a pure, steady, even exemplary existence while on the other he's becoming, because of his humiliation, quite free of the influence of public opinion, figuring it will look down on him no matter what he does. He begins doing what is right without caring what others may say and changes his mind about making a magnificent marriage. But he keeps on talking about his father's marvelous deeds . . .

Once, with his usual hard candor, he says, "The most important thing in the world is knowing the truth."

Then through a mixture of confidence and dismay, he mutters: "The whole truth and nothing but the truth."

Saqr Mowazeeni grows up the envy of his schoolmates because his father is a government official—a very minor one, true, but even that is a rare distinction in our neighborhood.

When Saqr graduates, he gets a job like his father's. After he's been working a year, his father dies, leaving no inheritance except a big family: his wife, his sister, two marriageable but dowryless daughters, and a bitch dog. He also leaves Saqr a deep-rooted tradition of devotion to duty and honor plus an unyielding aspiration toward a beautiful life . . .

Some time after his father's death, Saqr remarks to me: "If only Father had been a bum! My life would be free and easy."

Most of the neighborhood women earn some money in one way or another, but not those in households as respectable as the Mowazeeni's. They must wait and watch and feed off dreams. Saqr tries to support four women and a bitch on his pittance of a salary. Life locks its windows and squats like a stone.

Saqr's only outlet is to sit in the coffeehouse till midnight and whine. "My sisters won't ever get husbands. Only nobodies will ever think they're good enough, but we'll never let them marry nobodies, and *that* means I'll never have a chance to get married, not ever."

And in fact the whole family suffers from privation and thwarted desire, even the aunt and mother, both under fifty. But Saqr, an upright man in spite of his lusty vigor, simply longs for matrimony. "A small house, a wife, children: Paradise!" He sighs and his gaze melts down to sadness and dream.

*   *   *   *   *

Because he smothers his turbulent emotions so fiercely, the page of his face becomes pale and empty. As time passes, his lack of fulfillment erupts into spite for his family, himself, and his neighbors. Even his house takes on the plaintive look of bitter frustration.

To prevent gossip, the women, except when it's absolutely necessary to go out, stay shut up in the house, bored, suffering prisoners to tradition. United by shared deprivations and the everlasting struggle against despair, desire, and poverty, they entertain themselves by constant bickering. Moreover, they wage a secret, resentful war against their own poor guardian, himself no less downcast, no less tormented.

Even the bitch skulks uneasily in corners of the constricted house.

Since she might track dirt, she's almost never let out, so when visitors come to call, she gets overexcited, plays with them too roughly, hugging and humping their legs. When a bark sounds in the street, she goes crazy . . .

*   *   *   *   *

As he ages, Saqr sinks deeper into bachelorhood while the women wilt, foundering in an atmosphere soggy with black gloom. Throughout the neighborhood, Saqr, still young enough to make a life, provokes equal amounts of sympathy and disgust. This isn't easy to explain, but maybe he stands for spineless surrender to the decrees of fate, or utter flaccidity. And his face reflects every female anguish in his house.

One day I see his bitch dragging a swollen belly across the street and beam at her admiringly. "Well, at least you found a way to contribute some offspring to the neighborhood."

Saqr has already come to hate his family by that time and calls it "a family that doesn't know death any more than it knows life."

49

Every kid in the alley hopes The Night Visitor will come to call in his dreams.

He's real, no doubt about it, but his kingdom of light sets up its tent in pure hearts and pure hearts only. On feastday eves they tell us to take a bath, hop in bed, read the Exordium, and wish for whatever we want. "Let sleep take over. Who knows? Maybe kind luck will smile and send The Night Visitor to make all your dreams come true."

As I grew up, my wishes—fervent appeals from a heart secure between the hands of The Night Visitor—grew up with me.

"Oh Night Visitor, close the mosque school and get rid of our teacher."

"Oh Night Visitor, throw open the door to the garden of the Sufis and fill my lap with mulberries."

"Oh Night Visitor, get some urban renewal going around here."

"Oh Night Visitor, preserve us from poverty, stupidity, and death."

*   *   *   *   *

One day a splendorous procession passes through our alley, at its head a man immense in glory. Above the roadway crammed with gawking men, every window feels the filling squeeze of women. The air swells up with cheers and trillcries, shrillshrieking pipes and drumthrumps. The radiant man calls first on every small shop each by each, then enters the big ones, resthouse, saddlery, bakery, and bath. Into the mosque school and the government school he goes, into little mosque, cemetery, and courtyard. Then he checks out the old fountain, the archway vault, even the hash den and the booza.

His whole aspect awes me and sets joy boundless in my soul. And then an unshakeable conviction bombards me with brilliant light: this wonderful man is The Night Visitor, come at last to answer my silent nighttime prayers. So I pipe up in my childish voice, "Long Live The Night Visitor!"

What happens shocks me with surprise. The great crowd falls quiet, its faces turn stiff and sour—someone must have poured lemon juice down their gullets. The imam of the small mosque yanks on my ear and shouts, "You insolent brat!"

The caravanserai owner orders one of his guards to "get that little snot out of here."

Hands shove me toward our house as I break limit upon limit of shame and humiliation.

Silent and sad, I sit down with tears in my eyes. Then my father says, "What a simpleton! How could you forget The Night Visitor comes only in dreams?"

50

In an era now long gone, when the alley clung but barely to the swirling hem of change, thugs and bullies ruled us. The protection racket was the only force of order we knew. It was a kick in the teeth, yes, but it also meant dignity and pride; it was humiliation but also prosperity; it was pain . . .

Gaalus Dananeeri is one of the meanest gangsters in neighborhood history, a heavy drag on our lives. If he isn't in the coffeehouse sitting tall and solid as a mountain, he's out leading his retinue of toadies through the quarter. It's as if they're following a huge building. When I stare at him in obvious awe, my father practically jerks my arm off. "What are you, nuts? Mind your own business."

I ask if Gaalus is stronger than Antara, the Hercules of Africa. My father smiles and says, "Antara is only a legend. But this guy is for real, Allah preserve us."

He's a giant. His arms and legs reach out for yards and yards in every direction, it seems, and on top of a horse so high and so wildly he sways in the air, you think he's somehow held up from above. Sudden as quick wind is his attack, and he can juggle and twirl his club, emblem of his eminence, as deftly as any magician. In fights with rival gangs, his men know they'd better pitch in and help, not just stand there watching him bust enemies with his club and butt them with his head.

His vocal cords can't make any sounds except growls of wrath and screams of rage, and his small talk is a deluge of abuse. He calls his favorites "sons of thises and thats" and curses religion on his way home from worship. Even when he's soaking up extortion money or flattery, he never smiles, never proffers a single phrase of greeting. Everybody from the caravanserai owner to Hamooda the pimp is equal in his eyes—and not just as ripe prey for extortion, either, for often, in plain sight of neighborhood dignitaries, he farts or relieves himself, showing his privates.

One time a merchant comes up short and begs a week's grace, but Gaalus won't grant it. The man ends up hiding in his house with the women until Allah finds the money for him.

Another time, when the school principal punishes the son of one of his thugs, Gaalus and his gang stop him outside the school. They tell him to strip naked and walk home in the nude. The principal pleads for mercy, calls on the sacred names of Hussein and the Prophet, but Gaalus just glowers and waits for his order to be executed. The principle finally begins to take his clothes off, spilling more tears with each piece that falls, but stops when he gets down to his underwear. Dananeeri just snarls. Amid the gang's guffaws, the quaking principle at last pulls off his underpants and runs home trying to hide his secrets.

Gaalus scoffs at mere tradition; he won't scruple to make a man divorce his wife so he can marry her, and he's marrying and divorcing all the time. Since no one dares take up with any of his cast-offs, they're stuck with a tough choice between begging and whoring to stay alive.

Once he gets so sick he has to stay in bed for a week. His illness, a seer divines, is caused by all the curses various local people have heaped upon his head. So when Gaalus gets well, he orders us not to celebrate the Lesser Feast in any way whatsoever. We can't even visit the cemetery. The feast days pass over empty streets, closed shops, and silent houses. It looks like some vast calamity struck and threw us into mourning.

His reign is a time of terror, cowardice, shame, and hypocrisy, a season of nightmare, hushed moan and misery, an age of devils and scabrous stories, the heyday of hopelessness and blocked roads.

But on the other hand, the bastard cows the other quarters. After squashing the gangs from around the Hussein mosque, he destroys the Atoof mob and scares one from Darassa away. Jauntily and without a protective escort, our wedding processions wind out of our quarter; people scatter when they hear our footsteps, for they know that messing with us is asking for catastrophe.

* * * * *

This towering mountain was fated to fall in child's play.

Gaalus gets invited to a wedding in Al-Ahmar Street. A little boy comes up to him at the housedoor and says, "Hi, Uncle."

Gaalus, amazed at this bit of effrontery, glares down and says, "Whaddaya want, kid."

And then lightning.

Yes, with lightning speed the boy pulls a knife from the folds of his gallabiya and stabs him in the belly; then, as if trying to climb upward, he rips the knife all the way down to the bladder.

Gaalus Dananeeri freezes as if gripped by sleep. His guts slop out of his body and he topples to the ground like a building. With him falls all his bold power, all his brutality, all his confidence in himself and the order of things.

We find out later that the kid is the son of one of his victims, drilled by his mother in preparation for that moment of lighting.

* * * * *

The news tears through the alley like wildfire. We're appalled and horrified, we weep and we wail.

As the idea sinks in, the looks we exchange leak new feelings into our hearts: ease, peace, gratitude, joy.

When the dust settles, we decide we'd better mourn although we're happy, act mad although we're grateful, and try to avenge him though the satisfaction is ours.

So, in spite of our new weakness, we get embroiled in even deeper conflicts with our neighbors. Gaalus' death turns out to be as big as blight as his life. The wicked curse of his passage bedevils our lives for a long, long time.

74

51

Giddy with winter sunshine, I'm playing in front of our house. Across the street, Abdu the neighbor's son is also playing.

His voice is sweet, his face attractive and dreamy. I like to listen to him sing.

> By God you're strange and queer
> To flirt and call it fair
> To cut me with a glare
> While lesser wooers leer.

Abdu falls silent all of a sudden. His face grows sad for no reason. I think he's looking anxiously at me, so I ask him what's wrong. But he doesn't answer. Now it looks like he's about to laugh. But he doesn't do that, either. Instead, he falls on his face with a scream ripping out of him. His body goes rigid, his arms and legs shake, and he foams at the mouth. Good neighbors carry him into his house.

When I tell my mother, she exclaims, "May Allah be with him and with his poor mother."

Whispers say he is touched, that nowhere in all the wide world is there help for him.

He gets worse, sinking down to imbecility.

One day Gaalus Dananeeri is parading back from the cemetery at the head of his usual contingent. The whole neighborhood lines the streets in awe of him.

But not Abdu. He parks directly in the gangster's path and states, with nary a care in the world, "You aren't worth a good God damn, Gaalus. Up yours!"

Scared to death, I think, "Abdu has had it now."

But the monster grins, takes Abdu's arm in his, and walks him along quite peacefully.

Never before has this beast shown kindness or compassion.

This teaches me our alley's two sacred classes: gangsters and idiots.

So my childish fantasies begin to hover over these two possible vocations.

Sometimes I dream of the honor and glory of racketeering.

Sometimes I dream of the blessings of idiocy.

Zeyan the copper-polisher's helper stands at last exultant in the presence of Sanawi, our futuwa, our gangster chief, who says to him, "You say you're loyal. So what? Let me test you."

Zeyan replies fervently, "To hear is to obey, master of masters."

Sanawi calmly says, "Kill Um Ali the midwife," and orders Zeyan out of the room.

Zeyan is halfway home before he comes out of the fog. He slides into an abyss of confusion and mumbles to himself, "I never dreamed it would be this bad!"

*　　*　　*　　*　　*

Before this, Zeyan had been an obscure fellow in our alley, just one of many young men out sweating for his daily bread. But a searing love for Um Ali the midwife took shelter in his heart, never mind that she's a good twenty years his senior.

He took an objective approach to the situation and saw that every path to Um Ali was blocked. His prospects were strictly of the limited kind, and she would never take him unless he hit some lucky strike that turned his poverty upside down. It was then that he began to dream of joining Sanawi's gang, thinking that might be a way to leap the luck barrier.

He sent One-Eye Maimun, the Monkey, a friend of his father's, to speak on his behalf. One-Eye sang his praises to Sanawi and arranged for them to meet.

Now the audience is over—after one minute, just enough time for Sanawi to hand down that horrific commandment, "Kill Um Ali the midwife."

*　　*　　*　　*　　*

For a while, Zeyan follows his dazed face around the courtyard in front of the takiya, but God provides him with no way out. So, late at night, he sneaks off to see One-Eye the Monkey at the hash den. After kissing his hand, he stammers, "Dear Master, I'm ashamed of myself, but I just can't kill Um Ali."

One-Eye figures he can't do it because he doesn't know how. "What could possibly be easier? She's always getting called out in the middle of the night."

Zeyan cries out desperately, "But I want to marry her someday!"

"Aaaa, just kill her to prove yourself. You can marry someone else. Women are as thick as flies around here," One-Eye advises offhandedly.

"But why Um Ali? Why does it have to be her?"

"Because the boss said so, that's way. Can't be questioned. Maybe he even knows you've got the hots for her."

Zeyan sighs. "The fact is, I don't think I'm up to doing murder."

One-Eye gets mad, slaps him, and says "Did you think joining the gang would be a picnic?"

"I see I don't deserve the honor."

"Yeah? Well it's too late now."

"Too late?"

"He'll never forgive you for funking it. Your life is about to turn very sour all of a sudden."

As he trudges away from the hash den, Zeyan thinks of himself as one whose life is lost forever.

He tells his troubles to his mother. At first she suggests—but then earnestly urges—that he run away. So just before dawn Zeyan leaves home with fifty piasters and a vagabond's bundle, abandoning family, friends, and job to face hardship and the unknown.

And the time between his talk with the boss and his silent disappearance is but twenty hours in the lifespan of our alley.

53

Another extortionist who once ruled our neighborhood was Hamooda Halwani. They say he was unique because, unlike other futuwas, he actually retired due to old age and then lived to be seventy.

He repented, made the pilgrimage to Mecca, and spent his last days in the mosque.

His saga claims that one evening after prayers he was having a friendly chat with the imam and said, "Many people don't like futuwas, but a lot of them are good guys."

The imam smiled and said sarcastically, "Oh sure, and I bet your name's at the top of the list."

Hamooda responded quickly, "My good deeds shouldn't be underestimated."

"Fine, so give me an example, Muallim Hamooda."

"Remember that Ragab Al-Kol who was notorious for seducing

honest wives? It was I who arranged for him to die."

"But that's a crime, Muallim, a sin."

"Don't be petty and ridiculous. And I was the one who killed Samaa Denish, the guy who murdered his own stepson."

"But that was never proven. The court cleared him."

"To hell with courts. My heart, the best of judges, has always been my guide." Then, after a short pause—for talking tired him toward the end of his life—he continued, "And chalk up another one: I killed Faheema, the singsong girl and madame."

With a wince of disgust that escaped the old man's weak eyes, the imam said, "Yes, and at the time it was rumored that you killed her for reasons that had nothing whatsoever to do with her business."

"Don't believe everything you hear."

The imam snorted, "Please further increase my knowledge of your good deeds."

"I also killed Yamani Kheshi."

"What did he do wrong?"

"Oh, he was just too proud—walked around the neighborhood as if he'd created it."

"You mean he allowed himself to imitate his boss?"

"You're just too stubborn to admit I might have done a good deed."

"Don't get mad. Tell me more."

Hamooda chuckled through a mouth without benefit of cuspid, bicuspid, or molar, and then went on. "In fact my other murders can't be considered good deeds. But Allah has accepted my repentance anyway, all praise be to Him!"

After some hesitation, the imam decided he just had to ask one more question. "The weirdest murder story I ever heard was about Qerqoosh the slave. What happened that time?"

Hamooda laughed and begged God's forgiveness.

But the imam persisted. "Tell me, Muallim Hamooda."

The man who recalled all his crimes without feeling guilty said, "When Qerqoosh showed up at the cafe that night to smoke the bouri, there wasn't a thing between us. He smoked, drank coffee, and got up to leave. Then he said to the coffeeman, 'I'll be at your place tomorrow at the time we agreed on, to the second. Don't forget.' All I know is that I was suddenly enraged and decided to kill him on the spot. He never saw another dawn."

"That's all?"

"Nothing added, nothing taken away."

"But what made you so mad?"

"Beats me. I didn't know then and don't know now."

78

"But there must have been *some* reason."

"Maybe I was infuriated by his puffed-up self-assurance and faith in the future. He spoke from absolute trust and security. He was so cocksure about today and tomorrow."

"But there must be some other reason."

"Call it murder without cause if you like."

Thunderstruck, the imam stared at the man in wide-eyed wonder. Old age had made him feeble and left him nothing but his bones.

54

You can't hang around here long without hearing about this young punk named Abbas Gehesh. He's the type who doesn't know much of anything about anything. How could he? He takes a job, works a few days, and then gets the boot.

But one day he sees Anabeya Metwali, the popsicleman's daughter, and his heart so fills with the nectar of love he feels drunk. Clearly, he can never win her in any legitimate fashion, but, after a mighty amount of brain-cudgeling, he manages to come up with a scheme that may work. He enlists the aid of some friends of his, ne'er-do-wells to a man, and lays out his plot.

On the eve of Ashura, Hussein's feast, Anabeya goes out shopping. All of a sudden she's surrounded by a bunch of bums and creeps rowdy with obscene menace. Just then, Abbas Gehesh leaps from his hiding place on the fountain steps, a knight in shining armor. He pounces on the punks like a wild beast, flattens them one after another, and then walks up to the girl. "Now you may go your way in peace," he pants.

She thanks him and goes on, lost in admiration of his noble prowess. She makes of his deed a saga told by everyone.

As it happened, we didn't have a Big Boss right then, but the idea was far from dead. People were wondering if it wasn't about time to get the old protection system back in order again.

Somebody spots Abbas hanging around the popsicle peddler's house and shouts, "Hail to thee, Gehesh, Big Wheel of the Alley!"

This cheer gets Abbas all excited. Dreams play with his head like a football. At last, under the influence of drugs, he tells himself, "Hell, why not give it a try?"

After dropping heavy hints to pave the way, he gets his pals together and leads them to the cafe in a show of force. Since the quarter is in dire need of someone to stand up to other districts and protect it, people are glad to see a tough parade. They pledge allegiance to their new boss, Abbas Gehesh. The good-for-nothings become a gang and extortion money rains into their laps.

As their status grows, they swell with pride and walk the earth like camels, haughty heads high in the air. And little by little they come to believe their own bluff.

Abbas Gehesh asks for the hand of Anabeya Metwali, of course. Her father, face radiant with joy, exclaims, "How lucky we are! What an honor, O Muallim."

And though the marriage book is signed, no marriage can be consummated until a proper procession has taken place.

Just a shade slow on the uptake, Abbas recalls that the wedding procession of a futuwa absolutely *must* make the rounds of all neighboring quarters. This has always been seen as the ultimate test of the boss; he faces the challenges of all of his enemies and then goes back to a honeymoon bed and a futuwa's throne—or else proceeds, feet first, to the cemetery.

Well, whatever must be, must be. And who says luck won't serve him one more time?

So he and his cohorts drink themselves blind.

To the tunes of the oboes, with all the men in the alley for attendants, the torchlit parade rolls smoothly along.

Until it comes to Zuweyla Gate.

For there, at Bab Zuweyla, Boss Atoof and his henchmen block the street.

Abbas takes one look at him and the alcohol in his bloodstream evaporates.

As Atoof whirls and juggles his club like a circus performer, Gehesh's stomach plummets to his knees.

But when the crowd from our alley starts cheering with naive gusto, Abbas has to try to fiddle with his club, too.

You can't put off your fate forever.

Under an ominous silence, Abbas shuffles a few steps. Atoof walks forward gingerly.

To his buddies' amazement, Abbas rushes straight at the foe—but then, lightning quick, zips around the corner of Al-Hanafi Street and tears into the darkness like a bullet after a fugitive.

Everyone just stands there mute for a minute, all at a loss.

Then the whole square explodes in raucous shouts and guffaws. Abbas is never seen anywhere, never heard of again. His marriage stays on the books until enough time passes for it to be annulled.

Woe to us when district strife grows uncommonly fierce, when warring futuwas wrestle with each other.

Fear of sneak attacks fills our nights with terror. We can't even walk through other quarters without getting whacked and battered for no reason, and our wedding celebrations turn into gory battles that blacken the face of life and leave us miserable.

Our outlet to the great square is ringed with peril, but the back way, the narrow path along the graveyard, is haunted by fiends and muggers. We're cooped up like mice in a trap.

This a tale from just such a time.

*　*　*　*　*

Certain men whose judgment is respected propose a secret gate in the east wall. "Never mind about destroying a bit of wall," they say. "We can sneak into that wasteland of rocks out there, then circle back into town and go about our business. We'll be able to stop worrying about these rotten neighbors."

The ancient wall which lines the eastern side of our quarter rises close to the rugged Muqattam hills. We approve the plan and ask a local contractor to do the work. "But what if an enemy finds the hole and uses it to ambush us?" several citizens object.

"It won't be all that easy to get to, you know," retort the plan's adherents. "Between the hole and the nearest habitable area there's nothing but a rocky desert where no one ever sets foot. Besides, guarding it will be child's play."

So we get a path into the desert. Since it begins just behind the old fountain, we call it "Fountain Pass." Thus we make a secret opening to the world outside, avoiding the cemetery path and the great square that bound our alley.

One evening in the cafe, however, the geography teacher chirps out something new. "We think we're very clever and don't have a thing to worry about." His listeners are taken aback, even more so as he goes on. "You think feuds with other quarters are the only menace. In fact there's an enormous danger not one of you has ever even thought of." With a flourish, he adds, "And it's enough to wipe out the whole place in one fell swoop."

Urged to explain, he answers, "The danger is the gate itself."

"Fountain Pass?"

"Precisely. Suppose a heavy rain comes down out of the hills. The wall channels it right into that hole. It rushes in and drowns the whole quarter!"

Puzzlement and mockery rise in their eyes. "Yeah, sure. It rains about once a year and then it's just a bad joke."

He ignores this. "We're under those hills, we're at their feet. And this area we live in is a hollow."

Everybody laughs with derision. "So we forget a very real danger—getting our brains bashed out—in order to avoid a danger that exists only in your head? Get serious."

* * * * *

Passing years watch the alley struggle for its daily bread.

Once in a while the geography teacher repeats his warning, but it gets him nothing but sarcasm and the title, "Professor Falseprophet."

* * * * *

Then comes a bad winter. Heavy rain clouds pile up and then drop down to the very tips of the minarets.

The breaking storm blows everything off the rooftops and bends the mulberry trees in the takiya garden low.

Rivers flow from the sky. It pours three days without a break.

We've never known such savage cosmic wrath before.

And then from the hilltops, faster and faster, with the speed of a roaring train, agrowl with a gurgling surge under flashes of lightning and crashes of thunder, the torrent comes down, straight down our secret passage.

The earth vanishes under a rushing wall of water that rises higher by the second. It fills cellars, sweeps away our shops and businesses, floods all lower floors, overwhelms the school, and turns the small square into a deep lake. On the narrow path between the takiya and the old wall, a mighty river roars along, tears through the cemetery, rips corpses out of tombs. The lower places in the alley fill up with putrid bodies, shrouds, and clothes reduced to rags.

Whole houses collapse, roofs and walls become sieves, and everyone flees to the desert, homeless refugees. On every hand, utter desolation grips the earth and everything in it.

Disaster unforgettable.

Memory wet with tears.

Ambition toyed with the heart of Abdun the Sweet, a menial worker in the caravanserai. Like Zeyan before him, he decided to try to join the gang of Al-Duqma, our futuwa at the time. So he went to Ahad Kabar, a guy who knew his way around, to get some advice.

"Now if I were you," Ahad told him, "I wouldn't even get near him with that filthy face of yours, that smell. And just look at this greasy gallabiya you're wearing! Make yourself as clean as pure water, then try your luck. The Boss loves beauty and cleanliness, making him a unique link in the chain of bosses we've had around here. Get that through your head."

Sure that the road to Al-Duqma was easy and well-paved, Abdun trotted off to the bath for a new skin, buying a new gallabiya and a pair of slippers along the way. While he was getting all spiffed up in the bath house, a friend asked, "Hey, Abdun, what's up? Getting married or something?"

Abdun divulged his secret and the other man, a real friend, said, "Cleanliness alone won't satisfy Al-Duqma. He's a great lover of stories and fables."

"Fables?"

"Sure: Antara, Abu Zeid, all that legendary stuff. You can't talk to Al-Duqma more than a minute without a fund of fables."

"Collect myths and nonsense? But that'll take a long time!"

"Well, the storyteller sits in the cafe every night. If your heart's set on it, get busy. Don't waste your time around here."

As Abdun began to move away, his friend added, "Times have changed, Abdu. Al-Duqma at first accepted anyone who wanted to join, but now that he's sitting unchallenged on top of the world, he's choosy . . ."

Abdun was no fool; he saw it was wise to go slowly and patiently, to do the right thing. "It'd be dumb to get overeager and ruin my chances," he told himself.

So he held on to his job, worked hard, got married, and stayed up late every night at the cafe to sponge up tall tales told to the tune of the rababa. Life was neither comfortable nor easy. His work was strenuous. Providing for a family is no laughing matter. Learning all those old stories by heart is no small task. Abdun consoled himself by imagining his sweet dream: to stand before Al-Duqma in the purity of water and the richness of the rababa singer.

His secret got out and pretty soon everybody and his brother knew

Abdun the Sweet was studying to be a thug.

Many people, wise and good, counseled him. "Hygiene is important, storytelling essential, but to Al-Duqma courage is the most vital thing of all!"

"Courage?"

"Yes. But be careful. Don't let him start to envy you. He'll turn against you in that case."

"And how am I supposed to strike this delicate balance?"

"That's your problem. Solve it yourself. Use your noggin, Abdun, son of the Sweet!"

Another advised him: "Strength is very important. You have to prove you're strong, show you can deal telling blows, and demonstrate an ability to take blows no matter how hard. But of course your strength can't be comparable to his."

"But how can I do all that?"

"That's your problem, Abdun."

Abdun was getting mixed up, but, wishing for solace, he said, "Those in the know say he loves purity, beauty, and good. I myself bear witness that the way he treats the milkman proves beyond a doubt that he has an innate inclination toward good."

"And what about his treatment of the water carrier?" someone put in warily.

Abdun's heart shrank—but only for a moment. Then he said stubbornly, "My father once told me he loves the poor."

"I can name at least ten of the poorest of the poor in the alley whom he kicked out of their homes and tore to bits . . ."

Abdun came out of these conversations shaking his head in sad bewilderment. He even considered abandoning the road to gangsterdom, but the dream had mastered his soul and he couldn't let it go. His life was split into pieces: job, wife, storyteller, efforts of strength and courage, dreams of adventure . . .

Though his tenacity was tremendous, Abdun began to grow weary. He felt tied under some heavy weight. His foot began to slip, his grip on life began to loosen. He lost track of time, his mind wandered, and he began doing one silly thing after another. Somehow he managed to keep up with all his mad activities until at last he lost control completely. All his struggling proved fruitless: he got fired and, after a lot of wrangling, divorced.

He really didn't mind all that much because he figured it was about time to meet Al-Duqma, the only person left for him now.

The futuwa scrutinized him for a while, then asked him what he wanted.

"To be one of your servants."

"I suppose you think you're worthy?"

Abdun bowed his head to hide his pride in his elegance and attainments. "I have all the master needs or wants, plus more!"

Al-Duqma said dryly, "I don't need you."

The amazed Abdun pleaded: "For your sake I threw away my whole life!"

"I know," Al-Duqma said indifferently.

"And you brush me aside in spite of that?"

Impatient now, the Boss said, "I brush you aside *because* of that."

And the story of Abdun the Sweet became proverbial in our alley.

57

Zaghreb Balaqeeti was one of the most eminent racketeers we ever had, the last of the truly great. After him the protection game went downhill.

He was slender, tall, light of skin, heavily muscled, fast on his feet, and expert at flourishing his club. If it hadn't been for his conviction—a true one—that the authority and status of a futuwa could be established only by fighting, he would never have entered a battle. Well, he was lucky. He beat Darassa's chief to a pulp and just about killed the boss of Atoof. After proving his valor, he sheltered us in his shade like a tree flowering with pride and security. Everyone loved him, sang songs of his triumphs, and basked in his tender fatherliness. He liked to sit in cafes and draw all the rhymers, singers, and jokesters around him, the better to hear the stories. Even though I was quite young, I would give him greetings, and he would greet me back so politely I felt elated, full of hope. His attitude toward us was unprecedented and unique. He forced his followers to live by the sweat of their brows, and he himself sold dope wholesale, never demanding protection money unless it was absolutely necessary.

*   *   *   *   *

Still, the Boss is the Boss.

Zaghreb Balaqeeti's word is first and last on every subject. Benevolent oppression is bitter even if it leads to long life. Zaghreb warns men not to use foul language, tells women not to overdo it with make-up, and limits the games of children.

He butts into all kinds of things that don't concern him, even getting the rababa-bard to change the legend of Abu Zeid by adding verses that exaggerate his heroism. He stops marriages he thinks won't work out and prevents divorces even when both parties are dying to see the last of each other. When he's around, nobody dares ask for anise or caraway drinks because he hates the way they smell.

So despite his good intentions and kind character, one word from him puts us in chains. The situation becomes more critical every day because the neighborhood is getting more educated people, people with tender sensibilities and insolent tongues.

"Damn . . . Soon we'll be breathing on his command."

"He's a tyrant but he's just."

"The word 'tyrant' *means* 'unjust,' you idiot."

Unheard-of ideas pop up right and left. For the first time, there's a campaign against the protection game *per se,* regardless of its advantages. For the first time, people say it's an anachronism, that it's high time to let the police protect us. For the first time, a good futuwa is cursed as much as a bad one.

When these whispers reach Zaghreb Balaqeeti, he gets mad and shouts, "Is this the reward you give a man for being just and showing mercy, you sons of bitches?"

And he scowls and shakes his fist ferociously.

*   *   *   *   *

Some people look hopefully to Hagar the Hairless.

He's a giant, a pious soul, but a bit touched in the head. Once convinced that something is right, he'll head for it, heedless of any and all risks.

He sits at night in the small square in front of the takiya and recites Persian chants in mumbles to himself. A wily man sneaks up behind him and whispers in a gentle, moving voice, "Do you wish to serve Allah, Oh Hagar?"

Hagar believes it's a voice from heaven and cries out, "Here am I, Oh Lord!"

The man whispers, "To you were strength and power given to break our chains."

*   *   *   *   *

Hagar acts with the fervor of a man on a sacred mission.

The good people of our neighborhood fully expect the utter destruction of our prison.

86

Hagar shakes a huge club threateningly in the air. But then, all of a sudden, he clobbers the imam of the small mosque. He pounces on a woman and beats her up right there in the street. Then he starts bashing merchants, workers, and students.

The alley panics and goes mad. Shouts rise from the bedlam:

"Hagar's gone nuts."

"Arrest him."

"Surround him."

"Stone him."

And stones hail on him from every direction till he drops down in a pool of his own blood.

* * * * *

Nobody can figure out what went wrong.

Many people think he misunderstood the message or got mixed up, but others believe there's still some secret hidden somewhere in the affair.

Dissatisfaction with Zaghreb Balaqeeti keeps growing. People now speak loudly of things only whispered before—or never even mentioned. They fiercely resist the futuwa's attacks, and a rebellious spirit, totally new, spreads through the neighborhood. Several bloody and rueful incidents occur. At last the awesome position of Boss is eliminated and the gates open on a new age.

And somehow the story of Hagar the Hairless gets reborn in a new light, is understood in a new way, becomes, strangely enough, a symbol of the new life.

58

Spring finds us on the lip of the abyss of annihilation. Gang wars rage through the alley and the spite between us and other quarters screams at fever pitch. Rancor boils, hearts seethe with hate, murder lurks everywhere, and all our tomorrows stink of disaster.

Then at noon one sunny day, an inscrutable scene takes place on the cosmic stage.

Unseasonal clouds gather dark on the horizon, pile up, and grow so dark they smother the soul. Towering to the very liver of the sky, they block the light of the sun.

The clouds multiply, intermingle, merge, and slowly form up into mighty masses that build a roof of deep dark black.

From streets, shops, and rooftops, puzzled eyes lift up to heaven, every face in wonder open to the sky.

This dense black roof begins to roll, to wrestle, to heave like a sea of pitch fighting a horrible war.

People rush into the street to see this enigma, ignorant of what it might birth, afraid of something even more dreadful.

The air drinks blackness, grows yet darker, more ferocious, and then the sea begins to slobber long black tufts that fill the air and creep toward earth in eerie silence.

From all surrounding districts people run to the great square where they hope to find some small sense of security in milling around and touching others.

A noxious smell of dust inhabits our noses, reality disappears, dim demons hover over us—and then everything in the world plunges into pitch-dark murk.

Quavering voices cry, "Save us, Oh great God of grace!"

For an hour the awful dread of vast calamity engulfs us all.

And in that deep dark, hands reach out for other hands to clutch, and no one either knows or cares whose hand he holds.

59

Ghanam Abu-Rabyah's story is a weird one.

He was a man of humble origins even by alley standards, but he did well enough in school to land a job at the Ministry of the Interior. He climbed rung by rung to the position of budget chief for secret security.

His tidy home, pretty wife, tasty food, and respectable demeanor set him off from the ne'er-do-wells in his family, and everywhere he goes he attracts the needy like a magnet.

* * * * *

One day Ghanam Abu-Rabyah completely disappears.

People ask after him at home, in the cafe, among his friends, relatives, and envious acquaintances. Nobody gets a straight answer. His absence is shrouded in mystery, which of course leads to suspicion. He's not sick or away on business; he has no enemies, no connection with the ups and downs of politics. Suspicion hovers over the only things left, matters of extreme sensitivity, and each person works out a

90

theory that matches his own character and inclination. Some say he's simply run away, others that he's been murdered.

And then one day Ghanam Abu-Rabyah appears every bit as suddenly as he disappeared.

People crowd his house to welcome him back. He claims his disappearance was due to a personality conflict with a powerful official in the ministry. Ghanam had ended up slugging this dignitary in the jaw. He got arrested but refused to back down and was finally released.

This is widely believed and considered heroic. Ghanam goes into retirement ten years earlier than stipulated by law and is seen as a martyr. People are ready to distrust the Ministry of the Interior at the drop of a hat.

*   *   *   *   *

Some time later, a new story about Ghanam's disappearance begins to make the rounds. I don't know how it got started, what sources it had, or how much of it is true—and nobody else does, either. But in spite of all that it spreads quickly, solidifies, and becomes part of local lore.

They say—Allah knows best—that Ghanam Abu-Raybah took advantage of his position as supervisor of the secret security budget to embezzle ten thousand pounds (some say twenty thousand), that he got caught and interrogated, that he confessed.

Now this created an extremely delicate situation. Since he knew by heart the names of everyone to whom secret monies are disbursed, he could cause a tremendous scandal, shake the bureau's stoolies up severely, and destroy public confidence in the security apparatus for no good reason. What should be done? They asked him to return the money in exchange for a full pardon, but he turned them down flat. They arrested him in order to terrify him, but he just didn't care. No trace of the money could be found. They couldn't hand him over to the prosecutor's office because they were afraid he'd spill the beans to them. They kept looking for a compromise, but he wasn't having any. Dealing from a position of strength, he met their threats with mockery. "Thousands and thousands are spent every day on bastards with no morals. What's wrong with my getting a few piasters? The dust on my shoes is more honorable than the biggest chief among them. I won't give back a single millieme. I demand to be presented to the Attorney General."

Well, they couldn't keep him under arrest forever, couldn't even keep him in custody any longer without informing the Attorney General, so they made him swear to uphold the honor of the profession and follow its code while they, for their part, would stop asking for the money and accept his early retirement.

Ghanam Abu-Rabyah bought a vacant lot and built an apartment house. He was always considered one of the most notable men in the whole neighborhood.

60

Khaleem Rumana, one of our local young men, works in the copper shop engraving trays by hand. One day, without sending an excuse, he doesn't show up for work but is seen wandering around the small square in front of the takiya. He recognizes no one, not even himself, for when his mother gets word of his condition and calls him, he doesn't know who she is and acts as if he's hearing his name for the first time in his life, just like a newborn babe.

Everybody figures he's taken an overdose of something or other, but the thing goes on day after day and is finally accepted as another dreary fact of life. Rumana is an empty shell without memory or human contact, a living corpse. As usual, people say he's touched and recommend all the popular nostrums—incense, visits to appropriate shrines, and the giving of a zar—but nothing works. So they turn him over to Allah, the Compassionate, the Merciful.

*   *   *   *   *

One morning his mother spots a new look in his eyes, a living look asparkle with his former personality, which has, in fact, suddenly returned from a long journey. Her heart trembles with hope as she calls out, "Rumana."

Rumana squints anxiously at the angle of the sun rays coming through the basement window and says, "I'm late for work."

He hustles off to the shop and his mother cries all morning.

Rumana goes up to his boss and says, "Sorry, master, I guess I overslept. Please forgive me."

The man gives him a dubious look but guesses what must have happened and allows him to set to work. Rumana peers around the shop with evident concern, and, unable to find what he's looking for, asks, "Where's Bayumi?"

Bayumi is his best friend, the companion of his boyhood, and he's been expecting to see him as usual by him in the shop. But Bayumi's bench is empty and no one will answer his question.

* * * * *

Rumana gradually realizes that he's been gone for several months. He takes this in slowly and delicately but still can't quite figure out how to digest it. Moreover, he keeps returning to the question of Bayumi, his friend. Finally, someone gives him the pat answer of comfort to the bereaved: "He lives on in you."

"Bayumi's dead?" he cries.

"He was hanged."

"Hanged?"

"Convicted of the murder of Zenab the glass-bead peddler."

Rumana murmurs in amazement, "Bayumi killed Zenab!"

* * * * *

The few who know that Rumana has lost his only friend and his only sweetheart say to each other: "So now he knows he was betrayed in both love and friendship. They both deserted him, left him nothing but treachery and emptiness . . .

* * * * *

Rumana suffers another personality change. He doesn't retreat into blankness again, but *ennui* creeps into the depths of his soul, silence pitches her tent over him, and he lives in hate, spiteful and uncooperative. He wilts, turns pale, and falls ill with a sickness so grave he can't work. Everything in sight is black in his eyes.

To console him, his mother says, "You're not the only one who's had a bad time of it, you know. The disasters of this world are beyond count, innumerable."

Rumana leaves his house immediately and heads for the Gamaliya police station. Standing before the chief of police, he states calmly, "It was I who killed Zenab the glass-bead peddler."

Ibn Ayesha is the worthless type who lives by beggary and light fingers. He sneaks into Sitt Mashallah's house one night, sure she's at a wedding. But for some reason Sitt Mashallah returns. The next thing he knows, she's coming toward the bedroom, so he dives under the bed, all atremble with terror.

The lady's feet and calves come and go as she lights her gas lantern, and Ibn Ayesha hears her soulful song:

> Oh lover, if you would only come,
> I'd give this night a lovely hum!

He wonders when he'll get a chance to escape.

Sitt Mashallah goes away for a few minutes and comes back with four feet! He can see the green slippers and the hem of a striped galla-biya. Ibn Ayesha's heart turns to stone, certain his captivity will be a long one.

The lady says, "Welcome, bringer of light and joy."

A coarse voice says, "No one will notice we're not at the wedding."

And on the ears of Ibn Ayesha fall muffled mirthful whispers, smacks, and smooches.

The woman says, "He'll never guess I got out of that wedding crowd," and the coarse voice replies, "He'll kill us one of these days—if we don't kill him first."

Their love-making takes a long time.

Under the bed, the manzool Ibn Ayesha has taken numbs his senses, crawls up his lungs, and diffuses through his soul—in short, the usual opiate effects. Ibn Ayesha swims in a shoreless sea, then drifts up into space, soars in slow dream to a high peak and looks down on Sitt Mashallah's bedroom. He sees her in the clear lanternlight, sees her lover, sees the man beneath the bed. The naked woman undulates, a huge tree in a haze of gray smoke, while a monkey of a man plays in her branches. The game goes on and on, back and forth, back and forth. But a storm breaks over his hiding place, the smoke blows away, the leaves of the great tree begin flapping against each other, voices scream for blood, crashing and pounding fill the air, brutal blows are given and taken, smashing smacks from the heart of darkness that leave no trace of love . . .

To get as far away as possible from this nightmarish earth, Ibn Ayesha decides to continue his trip through space . . . . But he bumps into something or maybe something bumps into him.

It takes every bit of strength he can muster to get out of this grasp he's in, free his neck, and turn his head to the light.

Upon which he is dragged like a mat from under the bed.

He sways as he tries to stand still in order to see the amazed faces around him.

The sheikh of the alley says to the police officer, "This is Ibn Ayesha, a pickpocket, your honor."

"Well, he seems to have learned how to kill."

He's arrested, but the investigation doesn't convict him of the murder of Sitt Mashallah and her lover but finds and arrests the real killer instead.

So Ibn Ayesha lives to tell his story once an hour. Toward the end of his life, he's touched in the head, and it is said the Sufi madness fell upon him while he was under the bed of Sitt Mashallah.

62

Though Hag Ali Khalafawy was one of the richest men in our alley, he was much better known for goodness and piety than for wealth. He pitied the ill-treated, helped the poor, and was kind and generous to his relatives. His piety, compassion, and fear of God increased steadily as he grew older, and over a certain Maharan family he spread a benevolence that went far beyond the experience of everyone else who lived in the welcome shade of his kindness. These Maharans were dirt poor, and poverty had led them astray. They were petty criminals and thieves, notorious brawlers and bums.

When Hag Ali felt his time had come, he sent for his eldest son and said to him, "I had a dream, I saw a vision."

His son gazed at him in sympathetic suspense.

The pilgrim went on. "It's time I got this mountain of anguish off my chest."

"What dream? What vision? What mountain?"

Begging the forgiveness of God, the Hag said, "Appearances to the contrary, son, my life has been bitter."

"Kindest of men, why?"

The Hag had barely breath to speak. "I want to tell you about the Maharans."

"They get far more than they deserve from you. All they really deserve is punishment."

The pilgrim's eyes almost closed. "By rights, everything we own is theirs!"

Then he confessed that in early youth he and Maharan senior had been partners. They were traveling together when Maharan died. Ali stole his money. "And I invested it, and that very same money made us what we are today—just as the loss of it made the Maharans what they are."

His son was upset. "You don't mean what you're saying, Father."

"It's the truth, no more, no less."

They sank into a suffocating silence charged with anxiety till at last the Hag said, "My life was bitter. To save you from this curse, I want the money returned to its rightful owners."

"You mean we're going to admit we're thieves?" his son protested.

The father said in a tone of supplication, "That's your problem, son."

"No, Father, it's *yours.*"

"I've got one foot in the grave."

Dryly, the son asks, "And maybe you could explain why it never occurred to you to make restitution before?"

The Hag flinched and shut his eyes as if someone had smacked him, then murmured: "Oh God, extend my life so I can prepare myself to meet You."

But his prayer wasn't answered, no extra time vouchsafed. In fact, those who tell this story insinuate that his son helped him on his way by tampering with the medicines.

Well, that's how the story goes—embellished with accurate details only an eyewitness could possibly know.

But that's how stories are told in our alley.

63

Seeds of hate between Shuldoom and Qormah were planted in the flowerbeds of childhood; in the middle of a festival celebration, Shuldoom ripped Qormah's brand new gallabiya and started a fight. Qormah belted Shuldoom with a wooden shoe, scarring his forehead forever.

That may sound like ancient history, easily forgotten, but from that day on they harbored, each for the other, an ever-darkening bile of bitterness. Though games and neighborhood occasions often brought them together, the gluttonous germ still lurked and oozed its venom. The sight of each other became a powerful threat, an evil challenge.

In mosque school they goaded each other, tattled and picked on one another, tried to get the other in trouble with the sheikh.

When Shuldoom's father died, the mourning tent was put up as usual. Qormah perched on a nearby roof and sang that old wedding celebration tune, "Come to our home, golden bride, lucky groom."

When Shuldoom got engaged to the fishmonger's daughter, Qormah tried every trick in the book to snatch her away, including telling lies to her family. In the horrible brawl that ensued, Shuldoom lopped a hunk of Qormah's ear off, leaving a mark to make up for the scar on his brow.

Each married and had a child. Work kept them apart as they grew older, but the secret knot that bound them would not unravel. One Friday at worship they screamed insults at each other till the imam shouted them down with, "God damn Satan and all his allies!"

They became a local joke. People laughed at them—behind their backs, needless to say—but the snickers were a warning of evil events.

Success smiled kindly on Qormah and his life took a turn for the better. He opened a shop stocked with every variety of tobacco. Gold glittered in his teeth and flashed on his fingers. He claimed to have won a lottery and invested his winnings, but Shuldoom swore he'd divorce his wife if he hadn't embezzled his boss's money—if he wasn't, in short, a crook.

Shuldoom persuaded himself that he could get along in the world every bit as well as Qormah could and so let his hands stray into *his* boss's till. He got nabbed and sent to jail for several years.

When he got out, penniless and lost, and saw his archenemy thriving and rich, he went crazy. Every door slammed in his face save one: the racket. He broke into the game by storm and played it with ballooning lust for vengeance.

Qormah (now "Muallim Qormah") was his first extortion target. Qormah wasn't a nobody anymore; he was a reputable citizen with a big family he wanted to hang on to, clinging to life by clutching at the signs of it, so he began to tremble for his own life and the lives of his loved ones. He realized that to keep them he'd either have to make peace with Shuldoom or buy him off till he got a chance to blot him out.

Shuldoom played his game to the hilt, extorting money from Qormah without shame or limit or end. The situation became unbearable. Life became unlivable. Death was the only answer.

Qormah hired a killer to murder Shuldoom. But Shuldoom, a step ahead of him, decided to kill Qormah first. So he ambushed him one night and did him in.

But Shuldoom savored life but a little while longer than Qormah.

The hired killer murdered him to collect the rest of his fee from Qormah's widow.

That's how both men came to die on the same night.

*　*　*　*　*

After telling this tale, my father says, "Hate is of the devil, but men are a source of wonder."

64

Salama, the local cop, was renowned for honesty. We were so used to futuwa rule back in those days that we never bothered with trivialities like the law. But Salama was among the few who did respect the law. His incorruptibility and rectitude astonished everyone. Though he was as lowly as they come, the police chief and other officers couldn't help feeling proud of him.

He let himself in for an unimaginable ordeal by wedding an older woman, a widow with a full-grown son known to be a bad egg. The young man, Barhooma, made sure Salama would face a tough situation: he robbed a shop.

Salama, the alert, the ever-vigilant, caught him red-handed. He returned the stolen goods but filed no report, consoling himself by thrashing his stepson. But it didn't take him long to realize he'd squandered the very thing that set him apart from everyone else and made him what he was. He felt loathsome and disgraced, a man full of grief.

Meanwhile, Barhooma pushed his rottenness to new extremes. This drove Salama out of his mind, and he took to clobbering him every time he came into range. Barhooma got sick of this and told him, "Don't hit me, I'm warning you."

When Salama moved to the attack, Barhooma backed into a corner and cried: "I'll confess! I'll go to the cops and tell everything—especially about how you covered up for me. Touch me once more and I'll do it, I swear."

Salama was taken aback. He dammed up his anger long enough to ask, "You'd threaten me after all I've done for you?"

"Just hit me and see what happens."

"Then abandon your wicked ways."

Barhooma shouted, "Ha! I'm free," and ran out the door.

The remorseful Salama muttered, "I'm losing something invaluable, something irreplaceable, with every passing day."

He looked like he was falling apart and people noticed it. Salama began to feel they had changed toward him, too. They didn't take him as seriously as before and, though they still said nice things, their faces betrayed traces of irony. Before, their admiration had included some envy of his moral perfection, but now they wore smiles of compassion and mockery.

*　　*　　*　　*　　*

Salama put an end to his torment by confessing to the police.

The chief was moved. He ordered Barhooma's arrest. "And you, Salama, you can resign to avoid getting fired. Your fine record deserves that much."

Salama didn't stay unemployed for long. The owner of the granary hired him as a watchman.

His action was considered a good example by some and a species of idiocy by others.

65

The venerable Sheikh Labeeb is an institution in our alley. His face, like the takiya, the archway, and the ancient fountain, is a local landmark. Every day, squarely in front of the arch, he spreads out his sheepskin and takes up his post, in his hands a censer effusing aromas both slumbrous and rich. He wears a white gallabiya, a green skullcap, pitchblack kohl around his weak eyes, and a prayerbead necklace so long it lies in loops in his lap.

A crowd of women squats silently round him and awaits the next word from his mouth after they've cast their handkerchiefs. He mumbles, yawns, stretches, and at last manages a single word, "succor," say, or some famous proverb like, "Allah save the upright from future evildoers."

Each woman interprets his utterance as she sees fit. Her face brightens in joy or darkens in sorrow. She tucks whatever she can afford under the fleece and goes away.

And so for many long years money runs to this man, for his prophecies are famous and his name falls constantly from the mouths of the broken-hearted—and our neighborhood has an ample stock of those.

Sheikh Labeeb lives to such a great age that things change.

The river of supplicants becomes a trickle, a dribble. Schoolboys no longer venerate his sanctity but chase him around and jeer at him with taunting ditties. The sheikh yells: "Damn these new schools! Opened to teach nothing!"

He grows poor and his health decays. He threatens people with hellfire in the world to come, curses the age, and sighs with regret for the good old days full of good folk now long gone.

* * * * *

At last he yields to the times. He wanders around with his hand out, a beggar, crying, "All things earthly pass away."

66

Behind basement window bars a child's small face.
To any likely passerby he cries, "Hey, Uncle, please . . ."
The stroller stops. "What do you want?"
"Out. I want out."
"What stops you?"
"The locked door."
"No one is with you?"
"No one."
"Where is your mother?"
"Left and locked the door."
"Where is your father?"
"Left long ago."
The stroller sees what he wants to see.
Then smiles and goes his way.
Small behind bars, a child's face.
At the street, at people, looking with longing.

Outside every mosque there's a man who roams around with a censer, wafting smoke over people for a pittance. In our alley, it was Am Sukry, a poor man whose large family lived all crammed together in one room. His youngest child was named Abdu. Since he was the last grape in the bunch, his father decided to send him to mosque school. Abdu excelled from the first day. The sheikh advised Am Sukry to enroll Abdu in primary school.

Am Sukry couldn't make up his mind what to do. Should he put Abdu on the long road of booklearning or apprentice him to a tradesman? A student would be a parasite for many years while an apprentice could help the family with his wages. After some time, Am Sukry decided in favor of school, and Abdu's high grades soon dispelled his worries and fluffed his wings with pride. When Abdu graduated from grade school, his father beamed and said, "Now I have a son who qualifies for a government job."

This would have been fine, no doubt, had Abdu not insisted on going to high school. So what if he had to go in patched shoes, a greasy tarboosh, and a threadbare rag of a suit? His skill in discussing politics and his overall excellence kept his head held high.

Then he won a full scholarship to engineering school—and was then selected to study in England. From that day on, Am Sukry was called Abu Al-Muhandis, Father of the Engineer, and he became famous throughout the district, his son's intelligence a proverb. When he was young, Am Sukry had dreamed of joining the gang, being the futuwa, or at least winning a crucial brawl, but time wreaks marvelous changes.

* * * * *

Abdu comes to occupy a very high post in the ministry, and thanks to him we get electricity in our alley.

68

One of the most remarkable of alley tales is the story of Abdun Lelah.

His father pours beer for the denizens of the booza, and his mother sells pickled eggplant. Abdun is a baker's boy. He takes the dough from our houses and brings it back fresh-baked, quite an ordinary job, true, but Abdun isn't ordinary at all.

He falls in love with Selma, a streetsweeper's daughter, marries her, and lives in tranquil marital bliss. Vigorous and full of spirit, he works from dawn to dusk without a break, never gripes or grumbles, and wins the good opinion of his boss and the fondness of his customers. He prays every evening in the small mosque, attends Friday lessons faithfully, and makes a brother of the imam, always asking him for guidance when a problem comes up. He has no amusement except the bard in the cafe—and he even does the shopping on the way home from there, picking up a watermelon, some cucumbers, or a bit of dried fish.

With a genuine smile of patience, he politely puts up with his boss's tantrums, petty grievances from customers, and the derision of his friends.

What an oddity in our alley! It's as if he never heard an insult doubled and redoubled there, never saw a fight, never dealt with sinners and troublemakers.

*   *   *   *   *

He appears in the street one day in a new gallabiya whiter than milk, an embroidered skullcap, and red slippers. He hugs every friend he meets and kisses the hands of local notables. He doesn't go to the bakery and utters only one sentence, "The time is at hand."

He vanishes for a while, then appears on top of the archway. His calm and silent face gazes out over the whole neighborhood. Curious folk gather around the arch.

"How did Abdun get up there?"

"What's he doing in the breeding ground of snakes?"

"Snakes? That's the den of an afreet."

They shout up at him but he doesn't answer.

Then he jumps, smashing his head against the hard-packed earth of the alley.

And whenever I recall the death of Abdun Lelah, I tell myself, "Far easier to know why I live on than why Abdun jumped."

69

He doesn't go out unless he really has to and even then he scurries, wary fear in his eyes, deaf to the curses that fall on his ears, open only to what he wants to hear. He never goes through the archway or visits the cemetery. He lives alone in a basement room and has never married or given in to a whim or want of any kind. He lends out money at interest, a thing forbidden by the Prophet, and is called Abu Al-Makaram, Father of Generosity. Though people curse him, they seek him out when they get desperate.

When he reaches the age of seventy, he calls in his loans and retires.

He changes, exhibiting strange symptoms.

Through the basement window people see him squatting on the floor, face to the wall, motionless for hours . . .

He goes up to the imam one evening and just stands there before him without saying a word until the sheikh asks: "Why has Abu Al-Makaram come?"

Without preamble, he replies, "I had a dream." Not until he's pressed does he go on. "Someone came to me in a dream and told me to burn all my money, right down to the last penny!"

The imam smiles and says, "May Allah bring good things from this dream."

"But it keeps coming, night after night."

"What does your visitor look like?"

"I can't tell. When he's there, I have to squinch my eyes shut."

"Because he's so bright?"

"I think so . . ."

"Has he told you his name?"

"No."

After a long silence, the imam asks, "Can you give your money to the poor?"

Abu Al-Makaram gives the imam a skeptical look and walks away.

One summer day when earth and housewalls blaze with the fire of the sun, smoke rolls up from Abu Al-Makaram's basement. People rush to his window to see him standing there naked before a bonfire of money.

*　　*　　*　　*　　*

He's lost, a naked nothing scrabbling in rubbish piles for food, cowering in the dark beneath the arch. One day he is found there, dead, and is buried in the pauper's graveyard.

Then a certain rich man receives a dream visit from Saint Khudr. The saint reports that Abu Al-Makaram is one of God's favorites and informs the rich man that he has been given the task of building a shrine over his place of rest.

The man erects the shrine. As time passes, our collective memory of Abu Al-Makaram fades away until nothing is left except his being blessed of God.

I ask my father how the rich man knew it was Saint Khudr in the dream.

"Maybe he told him."

"But if Abu Al-Makaram was really one of God's favorites, wouldn't it have been better for him to give money to the needy?"

"If he had, we'd have considered him merely generous, not God's favorite."

After a long pause, he adds: "The dream is what matters. God gave him the gift of the dream. Do you have a dream like his?"

70

While peddlers sing out the sweetness of guavas and yams, autumn gathers clouds and casts dark shadows over the quarter.

Someone points to the archway and shouts, "God have mercy!"

A man comes staggering and moaning out of the arch as naked as the day he was born. His legs wobble, he collapses and falls to the earth, then pulls himself up by clawing at the wall. He looks around and weeps.

Decent folk hurry over to him, cover his nakedness, and find a deep gash in his head. "What happened?"

When he doesn't answer, they ask: "Who are you? What's your name?"

But he just groans.

"Where do you come from?"

No reply, no hope of a reply.

"Where are you going?"

Sheer guesswork says he's been mugged.

The wound heals over, but his mind is gone. He's one of the touched, living in our alley, never leaving it, trusting us for whatever help and pity come to him, fed by charity. In winter he sleeps under the arch, in summer by the takiya wall. He mumbles delirious words, laughs and cries without reason, and remains bereft of name, identity, origin, or purpose.

In our part of town, whatever excites disgust and disdain also generates reverence and respect, so after some time, Abdullah, Slave of Allah, a name for the nameless, begins to rise in station. A mystic halo of sanctity grows around him. People not only greet him and treat him with kindness, they're actually friendly. They even tell him their secrets and interpret his raving drivel, seeking his protection from calamity and the unforeseen.

One day I overhear a man defending Abdullah's "sanctity."

"We all know where we came from and where we're headed, and this has made our lives easier and better. Abdullah's life, on the other hand, has been made easier and given all its blessings in spite of his total ignorance of these things. Whoever enjoys the kingdom of life ignorant of his origin and purpose, ignorant of the meaning of life, is worthy of the reverence due to sanctity!"

71

A strange man in the coffeehouse.

A stranger attracts a lot of attention in our neighborhood, and we wonder where he came from.

Through the archway is the answer, meaning from the graveyard, meaning his footsteps are a bad omen.

The stranger goes into the corner and greets the imam, then says, "He who asks for guidance cannot fail."

"We advise by what we know, but true guidance is from God and God only," the imam responds.

"All I want is a little information about Yusef Murr."

"What for, brother?"

"Some respectable people asked me to do them this favor, so I came to you, chief among those who know."

The imam realizes he wants information for the parents of some young girl Yusef wishes to marry, so he says, "But he's already married."

"Religion makes allowances, thanks be to God."

"The Murr family has lived in these parts for a long time. Perfumery is their trade."

"How old is he?"

"Thirty or so. He works in his father's shop and has three sons."

"He sometimes goes away for a week or more?"

"You seem to know a lot about him," the imam says with a smile. "But he goes away only for business trips. Who has entrusted you with inquiring about him?"

The stranger answers apologetically, "I'm not at liberty to mention names."

The imam, annoyed, asks dryly, "And you, who are you?"

"I am called Abd Al-Akher, Contractor."

"What contracts do you deal in?"

"No, no, 'Contractor' is my last name. My job is grinding grain."

Then he makes his farewells and departs.

Word of this eventually reaches the astonished Yusef, who swears by God that he hasn't been trying to arrange a second marriage, that the idea never entered his head. Curiosity about the stranger and his secret flares higher and higher for a while, then fades out and disappears.

Then one evening the stranger comes from the great square.

He crosses the alley without pause and vanishes into the archway. He turns along the narrow path between the old wall and the takiya and walks on toward the cemetery.

When Yusef learns of this, he rushes after him till he is drowned in the darkness of the vault.

About an hour later his father begins to get worried, so, carrying a lantern to light the way, he and some of his workers set out to follow his son.

Under the vault, Persian prayer chants come to them from the takiya, and in the courtyard, by the light of the lantern, they find Yusef stretched out on the ground, empty of life.

The coroner later certifies that he died of a heart attack, but no one in the quarter believes this for a minute.

They shake their heads and mutter, "The stranger!"

But who was the stranger? And why did he kill Yusef Murr?

At this point, looks are exchanged, people remember that the name he gave meant something like "slave of the hereafter," secrets speak in whispers, and a wave of supernatural mystery rolls through the air.

72

Okla Issuramaty's story is indeed a story.

His father owned a circus, and Okla, even as a child, was renowned for his charming grace in the ring.

When his father dies, Okla quits the circus for no good reason. To prove how tough he is, he joins the rackets and makes a small fortune. Due to a mysterious something—some say an odor—that enflames women, he mounts the throne of love, tempting every heart. Other men get jealous, and one of the gansters tells him, "Behave yourself or I'll mess up your face for you."

But it's as if he can't know real love; he falls for a woman, then discards her. His conquests beggar the imagination, and it is said he has made a pact with the devil and learned magic.

Then he makes a sudden marriage.

The woman is a widow much older than Okla with nothing beautiful about her, but the way he sets himself up with her has an air of stability which seems to promise permanence.

He renounces the protection game just as he once gave up the circus, then opens a candy store and amasses a sizeable fortune.

In a few years this business bores him, so he closes it and opens a restaurant serving headmeat and liver. Successful again, he makes a fortune greater than the first.

A craving for possessions carries him away, replacing women, the circus, and racketeering in his soul. To feed it, he starts dealing in real estate and drugs. He buys a house and carriage and decks himself in gold.

One day he decides to move downtown, away from the alley. He builds himself a palace of a house and lives the life of the elite. After he buys a country estate, we never see him unless he comes down to consummate some big deal.

Traveling is next. He soon develops a mad passion for it. Travel so grips his brain that one day he's in Alexandria, the next in Aswan, the next Casablanca. He visits all the Arab countries and even makes daring forays into Europe.

Whenever a particular spot pleases him, he swears he'll never leave it as long as he lives, but he gets used to it, his infatuation dies, and he longs for someplace new. Love of travel makes him suffer just as love of women, things, and so forth had made him suffer before. Between trips, he comes back to our alley to see his friends and tidy up his business . . .

One evening, among friends from the drug trade, he asks himself, "What else can a man do?"

He tells them about his trips, but since they never set foot out of the quarter unless they have to, they couldn't care less.

And Okla asks himself, "I wonder where the Land of Waka-Waka could be? And the wall of the world—where's that? And if a man looks over it, what will he see?"

*   *   *   *   *

Rumor after rumor blooms around his name.

It is said he's become an alcoholic; it is said he's addicted to gambling; it is said he falls into follies beyond count and measure.

His absence lengthens until it is thought he will never again return. The community considers him lost.

Years pass.

One morning, in the courtyard in front of the takiya, the almost naked corpse of an aged man is found.

The residents of our alley recognize Okla Issuramaty. They peer at his body in bewilderment. Eternal silence and the hidden secret have cut him off from them.

His life was a legend, his death a slap in the face . . .

73

Mustafa Al-Dashoory, though the son of a water-carrier, is a schoolteacher, one of the few in our quarter with a solid education. He's my father's friend and is keeping him company one evening when suddenly from nowhere he says, "So tell me: what's the meaning of life?"

My father chuckles, but when he sees he's serious, dead serious, even insistent, he tells him what he knows about the beginning and the end, life and death, resurrection and judgment. Al-Dashoory says: "So you're positive about everything, life, death, and what comes after death. Do you have the slightest idea what happens in the tomb?"

My father explains about the prompter, the judgment of the two angels, the soul's resting place, and the intercession for deliverance on the last day, but Al-Dashoory interrupts him. "But do you know what happens to the human body hour by hour from death until it becomes a skeleton?"

And he regales us with a tale as horrifying and repugnant as a long nightmare, on and on until my father shouts in anger: "Enough! What are you trying to prove?"

"I just want you to picture a reality there's absolutely no doubt about."

"Don't you believe in God?" my father jeers.

"Yes. Nothing else makes sense. But," he continues after a moment, "God doesn't relate to us and I can't relate to Him. There is nothing but dead silence between us. I can't explain the evil in life and don't understand the weaknesses and inadequacies of nature. I have therefore concluded that God—praise be to Him—has decided to leave us to our own devices."

"Dangerous blasphemy, to put it bluntly."

But Al-Dashoory goes right on: "Therefore, belief in God demands belief in his lack of concern for our world, just as it implies that we're on our own."

"On your own?" my father yelps. "Can you imagine what people would be like if they bought this stupid idea?"

"Well, they could hardly be worse than they are. There's at least a little hope that they'd be better. People won't take life as a big joke, don't worry. They won't because they'll see it's a trust thrown down on us. You have to carry the trust in good earnest, you can't escape it without perishing. Yes, I know there are always a few profligates around, Omar Khayyam and Abu Nawas being prime examples, but it wasn't their philosophy which made their lives possible but the hard work of serious people who carried the trust for them. Besides, if everyone believed as they did, who would be left to supply them with bread, liquor, and gardens? So that won't happen. Mankind won't take life lightly just because God has left the world; there's no avoiding high resolve and new achievements, no escape from morality, law, and punishment. People might even begin to look to medical science for help in fighting weaknesses of thought and behavior just as they now seek its aid against physical disease. Don't worry. Their wills won't wilt away when they find themselves in a ship without a captain on a sea without a shore in a time without beginning or end. Heroism and nobility and sacrifice will never die . . ."

He rests a while, indulgent toward my father's exasperated scorn, then goes on. "And some day mankind will achieve a certain wholeness in themselves and in society. Then and only then, by virtue of this new human personality, will we understand the meaning of divinity. Its eternal essence will become clear . . ."

The argument keeps going till both are exhausted. Then, with genuine concern, Al-Dashoory asks, "What should I do to spread these ideas in the community?"

"The people who live here," my father retorts sharply, "are drowned in daily life, ground down by poverty, disease, strife—"

"—But these are the very problems my ideas will solve!"

"—and they understand one language and one language only. It arises out of suffering and supports them in affliction, it is consecrated by their vehement prayers to the Being you want to pluck from their hearts. Don't be foolish."

Al-Dashoory takes my father's advice, but in spite of his caution, outlandish notions are attributed to him, and his reputation among the people is ruined. An uproar erupts around him and drives him from his job. Life in our alley ignores him.

One-Eye gets ready for a love-tryst in the courtyard in front of the takiya. He decides to bolster his courage by downing a few in the booza, but he goes on drinking till he's plastered.

Melting with lust, he leaves the bar around midnight and fades into the darkness without any idea where he's going. In the blackness he bumps into Nono the madman, allowed to roam freely since his madness is harmless. Without recognizing him, One-Eye grabs his arm and says, "Guide me to the takiya."

Nono the madman starts walking and says, "Don't let go of my arm. What do you want with the takiya at this time of night?"

"If you really want to know, I'm off to meet my sweetheart."

"Fantastic! I'm going to meet my sweetheart too."

"You mean in the courtyard, like me?"

"Inside the actual takiya itself."

"But isn't the wall rather high for that sort of thing?"

"Nothing's impossible at night."

Since One-Eye has been staggering about and almost falling at every other step, he begins to gripe. "We've been on the march for a year. How come we're not there yet?"

"It's not a year. It's only a week."

One-Eye apologizes for his mistake and says, "You can't see Time in the dark."

"And the beloved? Can she be seen in the dark?"

"I don't need my eyes to recognize my beloved."

"Then you're mad!"

"OK, but where's the takiya?"

"You just admitted we've only been walking a week."

"But I can cross the whole alley in fifteen minutes!"

"Distance gets longer at night. Besides, aren't we still walking? Don't worry."

Then One-Eye gets dizzy and his legs fold up under him. He falls flat on his face in a dead sleep and doesn't wake up till sunrise. He looks around in amazement, for he finds himself right in front of the booza, not even one step away from its door.

*   *   *   *   *

And the narrator, a waiter in the bar, says he stood in the doorway listening to the drunkard and the madman talk and watching them circle each other and imagine they were making progress.

Thus a proverb is coined in our alley. Whenever someone asks for advice from a person who can't help, it is said, "You're drunk and he's mad, so how can you get to the takiya?"

75

Magnificent and utterly urbane, elegant walking stick under an arm, Omar Morgani enters the bar. A tightwound turban crowns his head, his white gallabiya radiates light, and his red wooden shoes gleam shiny and clean.

He salutes the gathered company with a cheery hail and says, "Let every heart rejoice and brim with bliss."

The very first swig stirs his innards and gives him the grins.

The second gulp produces total joy. He reels around in rapture and says to those nearby, "Believe me: in this world, sorrow is only a passing illusion."

He pours a third glass down his gullet and proclaims: "Damned be anyone who damns the world. A sweet snack, a sweet woman, a sweet belief. What more could anyone wish for?"

He assumes a graceful pose, twiddles his walking stick, and says, "My dear, good people, I am happy."

He then swings into a buoyant dance of joy . . .

All of a sudden a surly voice, source unknown, shouts at him, "How about letting us drink in peace!"

But he not only goes on dancing, he starts singing.

> Oh what a brouhaha,
> I've fallen for a fellaha.
> Oh what a mess is this:
> Captured by a peasant Miss.

The coarse voice retorts: "Have a little self-respect. Sit down and shut up."

But Omar Morgani remains in the arms of joy . . .

Then a club rises in the air, is flung at his head . . .

At that, he stops dancing. His warbling mouth snaps shut, his features stiffen as the pearls of happiness scatter, and he falls to the ground . . .

The news travels like a shooting star: the government is going to tear the takiya down for an urban renewal project. This becomes in an instant the talk of every shop, store, hash-den, booza, and vacant lot in the neighborhood.

"The blessings of the takiya protect us."

"Only the takiya has greenery and flowers."

"Song in praise of Allah is heard only from the takiya."

"Aside from the takiya, what place doesn't harbor harm?"

Considerable investigation turns up the odd truth that the originator of the project is the engineer Abdu Sukry, a native of our alley, the one who brought us lights!

Abdu says, "The takiya blocks the natural flow of the main street just like a dam and prevents us from expanding to the north."

Everyone else says, "Do you have any idea how much this upsets us? There's more than one way to the north, you know."

"But don't forget that the cemetery is slated to be moved to the Kafeer desert, leaving that space for full urbanization."

"Yeah, sure, Abdu. We've been hearing that one ever since we were born. And there it is, hasn't changed a bit, still in the same old place. But where on earth did you get the cheek to suggest destroying the takiya?"

The argument grows intense, feelings run high and hot, protests are written, and the whole community is swept by more anxiety and trouble than it has ever known.

Then a voice of moderation rises: "There's no reason to get all excited. Let's wait till the cemetery removal project is settled and work on it actually gets started. After that it'll make sense to talk about razing the takiya."

This opinion wins, the ministry retreats, and the project is postponed.

The majority, of course, rejects the whole idea out of hand.

The moderate minority says, "Let the takiya remain as long as the cemetery is still there."

77

Anwar Gilel is sitting on the old fountain steps laughing uproariously. Supposing he's either drunk or drugged, I go over and sit down next to him. "What's so funny?"

Through unbroken titters, he answers: "I've just realized that I'm a student among competing students in a school which throws together students from antagonistic little lanes, in an alley in the middle of warring alleys, that I'm a creature among millions of creatures both seen and unseen on a ball of mud awhirl amid a solar system over which I have no control, that this system is itself lost in endless space, that all life, myself included, is but a dewdrop on one leaf of a lofty tree, and that I have to accept all this and at the same time lead my life as if sorrow and joy were of any importance! That's why I can't stop laughing . . ."

For a long time, we laugh together, and then he peers at me with an ironic expression and asks: "Are you sure the sun will come up tomorrow?"

"I'd take bets on it," I answer firmly.

Still laughing, he says, "Blessed are the ignorant, for they are happy."

78

I got to know Sheikh Omar Fikri, a retired law clerk, through his visits to my father. As soon as his pension began, he opened a business to help the residents of our alley, for the connections between us and the big city were becoming stronger and more complex every day. From his office between the small mosque and the school he provided such services as renting houses, moving furniture, arranging funerals, and advising on commercial ventures as well as matters of marriage and divorce.

I heard him tell my father with proud self-confidence, "With my vast experience, I can offer services for any sphere of life!"

A craving long concealed boiled deep inside me and I asked, "Would you do a service for me?"

"What can I do to help you, my lad?" he beamed down at me.

"I want to see the High Sheikh of the takiya!"

Sheikh Omar laughed out loud and my father joined him. Then he said: "The concerns I manage are serious, related to the very essence of practical affairs."

"But you said you could do anything in any sphere of life."

"Don't you think the takiya lies outside the walls of life?"

"Well, no, actually, it's not like that . . ."

"Recite some Sufi poetry for us," my father said.

"My nightingale, *khoon deli khord wakuli hasel kared,*" I recited with joy.

Sheikh Omar Fikri said to my father, "Nothing is worse than repeating verses like this without understanding them." Then he looked down at me and asked if I understood a word of it. I shook my head. "They're strange folks speaking a weird language," he said, "but our quarter is all gaga over them."

Then I said to him, "You can do anything."

"Forgive him, almighty God," my father murmured.

"Why is it so important to see the High Sheikh of the dervishes?" the sheikh asked.

My father told him my old story. Sheikh Omar laughed and said: "Well, I guess I ought to confess that I once wanted to see the High Sheikh myself."

"Really?"

"Yes. I told myself, 'Here's a whole neighborhood repeating his name in spite of the fact that almost no one claims to have seen him.' I burned with desire to see him, craved it with the craving of a little kid. 'What stands between me and this wish?' So I marched boldly up to the takiya and demanded to see whoever was in charge. But from behind their wall they met me with grim, anxious looks and seemed very unwilling to understand what I was saying. When I tried to talk with gestures, they jumped back so startled and afraid I was sorry I'd bothered them. I saw I'd been stupid and went away in despair of fulfilling my wish by direct means. Legal penetration of the takiya was difficult or downright impossible and sneaking in was clearly against the law, hence not an option for a man whose life's work is based on respect for the judicial system."

"So you gave up your wish?"

"No, not exactly. I tried something else. I mixed with residents of our quarter great with age and famous in piety. A few said they'd seen him, but no two of them ever agreed on an accurate description. In fact, they differed to the point of outright contradiction, implying, in my opinion, that none of them had seen him."

"But I did," I put in eagerly.

"You aren't lying, but you *are* imagining."

"Why is it impossible to see him? Wouldn't he want to take an occasional stroll in the garden, for example?"

"But how do you know the one you saw was the High Sheikh and not just one of the dervishes?"

"That's a question you could ask any time. Is that how you washed your hands of the problem?"

"Not at all. I was crazier than you might think. I went defiantly to the Bureau of the Waqf and gathered a fair amount of information about the takiya's endowment, the particular order of Sufism they adhere to, and the dervish in charge of collecting the income. But I didn't hear one word about the High Sheikh except that he has miraculous powers, something our whole alley already believes."

I wilted in disappointment, glared at him, and said, "There must be some way."

With a smile, he answered, "Well, there's logic, which is what freed me from my feverish obsession. It told me that we see the takiya and the dervishes, but we don't see the High Sheikh."

"Can that be taken as a proof of his non-existence?" my father asked.

"No, it doesn't prove that, it just states what we all know: we see the takiya and the dervishes, we don't see the High Sheikh."

"But there must be a way to prove his existence and see him," I insisted.

"I don't believe it will be accomplished by legal means, and, as you know, I never stray from the law."

My father laughed and said, "So, Sheikh Omar, you have to admit there's at least one service you can't perform."

"So be it. But what's the use of seeing the High Sheikh? Wasn't it a silly wish?"

Then I asked him heatedly, "Why do they slam the gate in our faces?"

"The takiya was originally built in the open because this order sings of seclusion, isolation from people and the world, but as time passed the city overtook and surrounded them with the living and the dead. As a last resort, they closed their doors to attain solitude."

He smiled a lukewarm smile. "I've given you all the information you could possibly want. It may be useless for the fulfillment of your wish, but at least it makes it clear that you can't fulfill it without breaking the law."

*   *   *   *   *

This is an unforgettable memory.

To this very day I've never been able to muster enough courage to break the law, but, at the same time, I can't imagine a takiya without a High Sheikh.

As days go by, I stop looking at the takiya except when we pass it to visit the tombs. Then I throw it a smiling glance and let a few memories come back. I try to remember the figure of the Sheikh—or whoever it was I once upon a time thought was the Sheikh—and then I just go on along the narrow path leading to the cemetery.

Glossary

afreet: An evil, powerful demon.

alma: A singer, a chanteuse.

booza: A place where a beer-like beverage of the same name is consumed.

bouri: A water pipe.

dallala: A middlewoman, brokeress, or go-between.

dervish: A name for a member of some of the more ecstatic Sufi sects.

Exordium: "The Opening" or first chapter of the Quran: "In the name of God, the Merciful, the Compassionate. Praise be to God, Lord of the Worlds, Merciful, Compassionate, Master of the Day of Doom. Thee alone do we serve, to Thee alone cry for help. Guide us in the straight path, the path of those blessed by thee, not of those with whom Thou art angry, not of those who stray."

falafel: Fried bean paste, herbs, and spices.

fellah, fellahah, fellaheen: masculine, feminine, and plural of the word for "peasant."

Fo'ad, Sultan (King of Egypt from 1922 until his death in 1936): Member of the Turkish royal family that ruled Egypt for many years. Because he fought the Wafd, Saad Zaghloul's party, in order to keep his power from being eroded after British rule ended, he was seen as antinationalist and collaborationist during the struggle for independence.

futuwa: A gangster leader.

gallabiya: The long, loose, beltless, one-piece outer robe worn by men and women alike in many Middle Eastern societies.

ghurza: A hashish den.

hanteet: A slang word for an herb unknown to English, valued because it is thought to be good for what ails you.

helwa: Sweets, candy, or confections.

hookah: A large water pipe often used to smoke tobacco.

imam: The man who stands in front of others in the mosque to lead the formal prayers.

jinn: Invisible demons believed capable of interfering with human affairs for both good and evil.

kanoon: A musical instrument somewhat like a zither.

leban: A coagulated sour milk snack.

malaya: A long black headdress and shoulder wrap worn by women.

manzool: A mixture of smokable hallucinogenics and opiates.

mashta: A hairdresser or beautician.

millieme: The thousandth part of an Egyptian pound.

muallim: A teacher, master, instructor, and, by extension, a person worthy of respect.

nay: A bamboo flute.

oud: A musical instrument somewhat like a mandolin.

piaster: The hundredth part of an Egyptian pound.

rababa: A two-stringed instrument resembling a violin.

riq: A tambourine.

sheikh: A master, a teacher of religion, an elder or patriarch, an elderly, venerable gentleman, a chief, or the head of a tribe.

Sufi: A member of one of the many mystic sects of Islam which emphasize the seeking of a direct experience with God. The Sufis have often come into conflict with the more traditional and legalistic forms of orthodox Islamic law and practice.

sura: General name for any chapter of the Quran.

takiya: A monastery for a Muslim order, usually of ascetic Sufis.

waqf: An endowment to a religious institution which may, after a certain time, become an inheritance to heirs of the endower if so established.

Waka-Waka, Land of: A sort of never-never land often mentioned in children's stories.

Zaghloul, Saad: An Egyptian leader who stood for complete independence from Great Britain; he was the center of Egyptian patriotism from World War I until his death in 1927.

zar: A rite of exorcism.